CW00613524

PRAISE FOR M.

A fabulous soaring thriller.

— *Take Over at Midnight*, Midwest Book Review

Meticulously researched, hard-hitting, and suspenseful.

— *Pure Heat*, Publishers Weekly, starred review

Expert technical details abound, as do realistic military missions with superb imagery that will have readers feeling as if they are right there in the midst and on the edges of their seats.

— *Light Up the Night*, RT Reviews, 4 1/2 stars

Buchman has catapulted his way to the top tier of my favorite authors.

— Fresh Fiction

Nonstop action that will keep readers on the edge of their seats.

— *Take Over at Midnight*, Library Journal

M L. Buchman's ability to keep the reader right in the middle of the action is amazing.

— Long and Short Reviews

The only thing you'll ask yourself is, "When does the next one come out?"

— *Wait Until Midnight,* RT Reviews, 4 stars

The first...of (a) stellar, long-running (military) romantic suspense series.

— *The Night is Mine,* Booklist, "The 20 Best Romantic Suspense Novels: Modern Masterpieces"

I knew the books would be good, but I didn't realize how good.

— Night Stalkers series, Kirkus Reviews

Buchman mixes adrenalin-spiking battles and brusque military jargon with a sensitive approach.

— Publishers Weekly

13 times "Top Pick of the Month"

— Night Owl Reviews

Tom Clancy fans open to a strong female lead will clamor for more.

Superb! Miranda is utterly compelling!

Miranda Chase continues to astound and charm.

Escape Rating: A. Five Stars! OMG just start with *Drone* and be prepared for a fantastic binge-read!

The best military thriller I've read in a very long time. Love the female characters.

UNDERWATER
CHRISTMAS

A SUBMARINE RACE ROMANCE STORY

M. L. BUCHMAN

Other works by M. L. Buchman: *(* - also in audio)*

Action-Adventure Thrillers

Dead Chef
One Chef!
Two Chef!

Miranda Chase
Drone*
Thunderbolt*
Condor*
Ghostrider*
Raider*
Chinook*
Havoc*
White Top*
Start the Chase*

Science Fiction / Fantasy

Deities Anonymous
Cookbook from Hell: Reheated
Saviors 101

Single Titles
Monk's Maze
the Me and Elsie Chronicles

Contemporary Romance

Eagle Cove
Return to Eagle Cove
Recipe for Eagle Cove
Longing for Eagle Cove
Keepsake for Eagle Cove

Love Abroad
Heart of the Cotswolds: England
Path of Love: Cinque Terre, Italy

Where Dreams
Where Dreams are Born
Where Dreams Reside
Where Dreams Are of Christmas*
Where Dreams Unfold
Where Dreams Are Written
Where Dreams Continue

Non-Fiction

Strategies for Success
Managing Your Inner Artist/Writer
Estate Planning for Authors*
Character Voice
Narrate and Record Your Own
Audiobook*

Short Story Series by M. L. Buchman:

Action-Adventure Thrillers

Dead Chef

Miranda Chase Origin Stories

Romantic Suspense

Antarctic Ice Fliers

US Coast Guard

Contemporary Romance

Eagle Cove

Other

Deities Anonymous (fantasy)

Single Titles

The Emily Beale Universe
(military romantic suspense)

The Night Stalkers
MAIN FLIGHT
The Night Is Mine
I Own the Dawn
Wait Until Dark
Take Over at Midnight
Light Up the Night
Bring On the Dusk
By Break of Day
Target of the Heart
Target Lock on Love
Target of Mine
Target of One's Own
NIGHT STALKERS HOLIDAYS
*Daniel's Christmas**
*Frank's Independence Day**
*Peter's Christmas**
Christmas at Steel Beach
*Zachary's Christmas**
*Roy's Independence Day**
*Damien's Christmas**
Christmas at Peleliu Cove

Henderson's Ranch
*Nathan's Big Sky**
*Big Sky, Loyal Heart**
*Big Sky Dog Whisperer**
*Tales of Henderson's Ranch**

Shadow Force: Psi
*At the Slightest Sound**
*At the Quietest Word**
*At the Merest Glance**
*At the Clearest Sensation**

White House Protection Force
*Off the Leash**
*On Your Mark**
*In the Weeds**

Firehawks
Pure Heat
Full Blaze
*Hot Point**
*Flash of Fire**
Wild Fire
SMOKEJUMPERS
*Wildfire at Dawn**
*Wildfire at Larch Creek**
*Wildfire on the Skagit**

Delta Force
*Target Engaged**
*Heart Strike**
*Wild Justice**
*Midnight Trust**

Emily Beale Universe Short Story Series
The Night Stalkers
The Night Stalkers Stories
The Night Stalkers CSAR
The Night Stalkers Wedding Stories
The Future Night Stalkers

Delta Force
Th Delta Force Shooters
The Delta Force Warriors

Firehawks
The Firehawks Lookouts
The Firehawks Hotshots
The Firebirds

White House Protection Force
Stories

Future Night Stalkers
Stories (Science Fiction)

The Emily Beale Universe
Reading Order Road Map

any series and any novel may be read stand-alone
(all have a complete heartwarming Happy Ever After)

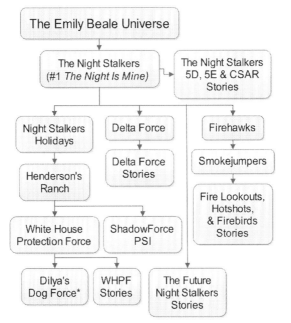

The Emily Beale Universe

The Night Stalkers
(#1 *The Night Is Mine*)

The Night Stalkers
5D, 5E & CSAR
Stories

Night Stalkers
Holidays

Delta Force

Firehawks

Henderson's
Ranch

Delta Force
Stories

Smokejumpers

White House
Protection Force

ShadowForce
PSI

Fire Lookouts,
Hotshots,
& Firebirds
Stories

Dilya's
Dog Force*

WHPF
Stories

The Future
Night Stalkers
Stories

* Coming soon
For more information and alternate reading orders, please
visit: www.mlbuchman.com/reading-order

ABOUT THIS BOOK

WHEN CAN A COLLEGIATE SUBMARINE CHALLENGE BECOME A **race for a woman's dreams?**

Malee Ashoona, born and raised in Nome, Alaska, leaves her state for the first time. Why? To join in the International Submarine Races in Maryland. When her team leader disappears, the pressure mounts until she's forced to take the helm.

Vlad Qarpik was raised two hundred miles from Nome, on Russia's Chukchi Peninsula. His path to the ISR has led him through Moscow and France to join the races. Finding Malee and their shared culture is a winning prize of its own.

When disaster strikes, can they follow a new course together before it sinks out of sight?

1

GLARING AT FRANK KOOTOO'S BACK ISN'T KILLING HIM. MY scowls never killed so much as a goldfish, but I keep hoping. Not exactly the Christmas spirit, but I'm past caring.

I don't know why I try, even Kryptonite couldn't kill someone like Kootoo. And confronting his ego directly would bring a whole world of pain I've got zero interest in. Especially not here and now.

Still, if he falls over dead in the immediate future I'll do a happy chicken dance. Or maybe a successful-walrus-hunt dance. Aanaa and Aataa are very traditional after all and they'd appreciate the irony. They tried to instill some of that in us grandkids, though maybe dancing on Kootoo's grave wasn't what they had in mind when passing on their traditions.

Of course my last year had been anything but traditional, especially by our hometown's standards. How many Inuit girls in Nome spent the last year designing a human-powered submarine? One. Me. No boys either, if I'm counting.

Most of my work was remote, virtual connections with

the three others of our team at the University of Alaska, Fairbanks campus. That's where Frank Kootoo browbeat Carol and Kane into working with him.

And Malee makes four. Lucky me.

We're the only team without their professor, but he's down with a horrid flu, and we're here with only ourselves to count on. Still, we *are* here and the ISR, International Submarine Races, are on—which is great.

It was only the third time I'd met the team in person and Kootoo is proving to have eight more kinds of horrible in person than I ever knew. Like snow, there should be a name for every type of horrible he embodies: officious, know-it-all, smart enough that he might at least know-most, arrogant beyond belief, takes offense at imaginary...

Maybe he's been culturing new kinds just for this occasion. If so, he's an expert. But seeking the perfect eight, or eight hundred, words to describe his horriblitude only makes me think more about him when I'm trying so hard to think less.

To distract myself, I look around at all of the other submarine design teams that are gathered in the parking lot for the pre-competition photo shoot. The shoot is done now and the teams are starting to check each other out. Not our team, of course, because Kootoo has already alienated everyone nearby.

He even managed to tick off Tricky Gal the sniffer dog and her handler Bethany as we and our gear were checked for explosives. The ISR is held on a Navy base in Potomac, Maryland, so of course there's security. Only Kootoo took it personally.

Tricky never growls at anyone, Bethany had spoken in surprise as she sought to calm her German Shepherd.

She'll growl less after I've turned her into fishbait, was Kootoo's piss-off-anyone-you-can response.

Twenty-six universities from all over the world had sent teams here, hoping for a win from the Foundation of Underwater Research and Education. About half of the submarines are one-person craft, though few as tiny as ours, designed with minimal water displacement in mind. The others are big enough for two powerful athletes to be powering the drivetrain. Though MIT's massive, sixteen-foot boat is crazy to look at.

Finesse versus brute force, I still like the choices I made as our hydrodynamics designer. The overall design and the impeller are mine. Carol and Kane were the builders, and Kootoo browbeat the U of A into financing us with the very best materials. He made sure that we received everything we needed from Kevlar for building the hull to custom aluminum castings for the drivetrain to personalized athletic training for me as the backup driver. Even though he's the sophomore to us three seniors, his skills as a project manager are unquestionable.

His skills as a human being are *highly* questionable— evil space alien in a Kootoo suit. I keep waiting for the *Men in Black* to show up and exterminate him, but Will Smith never does, which is too bad; I'd love to meet him.

I smile at my own joke, which Kootoo turns in time to spot and scowl at.

I wait until he turns away again to resume my useless death-ray scowl. He reaches around to brush at one of his shoulder blades. For half a second I wonder if it's working, then I notice that he's brushing his shoulder with his middle finger just for me. If it was anyone else, I'd bet they were smiling and making a joke. Not our resident evil spirit.

It's still the first morning of the five-day event, and

Kootoo has already alienated nine of the teams, three judges, and every other person he has come in contact with. He achieved all that before they'd finished checking in the teams. By the end of the competition? I make sure that my sigh is silent.

At first we other three teammates received sympathetic eye rolls from the judges, but even those are happening less and less already. Day One, Morning One, and us, the U of A Nanooks, are not only the smallest crew but also the outcast crew.

"You have the bad draw," a thick Russian voice whispered from close by my ear. His hidden laugh is almost as rich as his accent.

The whisperer is wearing a Grenoble INP Institut d'ingénierie t-shirt. He's not a big man, only a few centimeters over my own height. But he's the only other person of the hundreds here who looks like me or Frank Kootoo. His skin a shade lighter than my dusky Native coloring, but he has the prominent cheekbones, narrow eyes, and long face of my own people.

"The very bad luck of the draw," I reply...after checking that Kootoo is well out of earshot. He's on the other side of the crowded parking area scowling at the University of Washington's entry and will be annoying their team past reason within seconds.

"I fix this. Come." He snags my arm and leads me toward the people-sized door between the closed roll-up garage doors without asking. Massive US Navy-blue letters above the doors declare *David Taylor Model Basin*. A giant wreath below the name marks that Christmas is fast approaching. Many of the teams are shivering, but Maryland is thirty degrees warmer than Nome and forty above Fairbanks this time of year. Not a single Nanook has zipped their parka; it's barely freezing.

My Russian from Grenoble, France guides me with a half smile that dares me to yank my arm free and return to face whatever new disaster Kootoo is creating.

"Fine. So fix it already."

"Oh, him? No. I don't fix him. I fix you."

I plant my feet firmly which pulls my arm free from his grasp. "I don't need fixing." I know he was flirting with me, a lot of boys do that and I'm fine with flirting back. But I like me the way I am. Mother often forgets that I'm twenty, not seven, but she is the only one I let get away with that.

"Sure you do," he gets behind me and shoos me forward like coaxing a seal pup back to its mother. "You need to join my tour group so that you are away from the bad luck draw for long enough to remember where you are."

I look at the building once more. He's right. I made it here, which is *beyond* amazing.

The scientists and operators of the DTMB are indeed putting together tour groups. The submarine teams range from our four-person squad of Nanooks, to massive eighteen-person teams from Cal Tech, MIT, and the University of Vancouver. Mixed groups of thirty at a time are being led inside. It was with only a minor pang of guilt that I leave Carol and Kane to deal with Frank Kootoo.

He's merely awful to them; for me he has a special barb in his soul. Like he'd be happier if a seal harpoon suddenly sprouted from my chest—starting from my back. For at least several tenths of a second I weigh the unknown Russian's smile against having a break from being Kootoo's primary target, then wave for him to lead the way.

Besides, I've spent a year *dreaming* of walking into this building.

I had studied the DTMB as much as possible, but the reality is so much more.

"Built in 1938," our group's tour leader announces, "the David Taylor Model Basin is the largest of its kind in the world. This basin and its predecessor, built in 1896, have been the testing pool for almost every major US hull design in the last hundred and twenty years. We do water testing for ships and submarines—both military and commercial. The bulbous forefoot on world's largest cargo and cruise ships was developed here. Ships, destroyers, aircraft carriers, and even patrol boats were first built as models and tested here. Even many generations of America's Cup sailing boats. However, any rumors that we did underwater testing for Santa's sleigh to deliver Christmas to submarines on patrol will neither be confirmed nor denied."

He earns his laugh, then keeps rattling on about the history I already know as I try to take it all in.

The building is a kilometer long and shaped like a road tunnel—a half-pipe of concrete arcs above us. No windows. "Blocking the sunlight keeps down algae growth in the pool," our guide tells us. Lights are generally low, giving the tunnel-shaped space a shadowed, mysterious feel. Christmas lights do add cheer though.

The pool itself is well lit and it's the whole reason DTMB exists.

Fifteen meters wide and varying from three to seven meters deep. Nine hundred meters long, it holds twenty-five Olympic swimming pools worth of water. The *singular* swimming pool in Nome is only one-quarter of an Olympic pool, and uses salt water rather than fresh. I can only hope that my model testing holds up. Extrapolating from a carved block of wood with some added metal weights, that I dragged around the pool at the end of a handheld fish scale as a dynamometer to test drag, to a computer model, and then to a finished submarine could be a total fiasco. The actual tests of the finished submarine in the University of Alaska, Fairbanks, Patty Pool weren't much more helpful as it was only half-Olympic in size.

The tour guide continued, "Special carriages run above the water—on stainless steel tracks that are arced by five centimeters, that's two inches—along the whole length of the pool. We do this, because the water's surface curves that much in a kilometer to match the curvature of the Earth. We can move a model through the water at a constant depth of immersion, and run at speeds of up to fifty knots, on the surface or submerged. It's all fully instrumented so that we can study hull flow, cavitation, and any other necessary properties. Your submarines will be moving much slower, of course."

Omer II holds the record of traveling the length of the pool at 6.85 knots, 7.9 miles per hour. The École de technologie supérieure (ÉTS) team from Montreal is back this year and I so want to beat them.

Yes, I want the Speed Award.

I'd love the Overall Design Award, but have given that up seeing some of the other subs. Our sub looks cobbled by comparison with several others that look like they were built at a Naval shipyard they're so perfect.

What I *covet* is the Innovation Award; but that is also probably out of my reach.

Before the races have even started, we've already placed last in the Best Team Spirit Award, so I decide not to worry about that one.

The rest of the tour is a blur as I wish for the Christmas present of winning at least the Speed Award. Maybe even taking over the world record in the process.

The guide leads us down a flight of stairs to the big windows at mid-pool so that each passing craft can be observed from the side as well. At the far end is a forty-meter square tank for testing hulls during turns. Through a metal door into an adjacent warehouse there are towering racks of the models that have been built and tested here. They range from a meter long to massive ten-meter ones for detailed testing of the biggest ship designs. We breeze past them in thirty seconds. I wish I could find the designer of each one to spend a day discussing what they learned.

The Russian gave me his name, which I instantly forgot. Or maybe I never heard. No, we must have exchanged names because he's used mine several times.

His running commentary of small jokes doesn't let me forget about him. As we return down one side of the pool, I can see Kootoo in another group going the opposite way on the other side.

There is a large bubble of empty space around him. No surprise there.

He's glaring Ahab-sized harpoons at me. No surprise there either.

"How can one person be so offensive?"

"Years of practice, Malee Ashoona," my Russian friend jokes. "Years of practice." He always says my last name as if it is somehow more important than my first.

That's when I finally think to look at his ID badge: Vlad Qarpik.

I know several Qarpiks. They have visited Nome from across the *Ice Curtain* of the Bering Sea. For most of the last thirty years since the collapse of the Soviet Union, Alaska natives and those of Russia's Chukchi Peninsula can visit relations without expensive and difficult to obtain visas. My grandparents renewed old friendships with several of the Russian families including the Qarpiks.

I *should* like Vlad for my grandparents' sake; a task that I decide won't be difficult at all. When I switch our conversation from English to Inuktitut, his Russian accent is almost undetectable.

2

Our entry is the *Nanook*—Kootoo insisted that our submarine be the *Polar Bear* after the University of Alaska Nanook mascot because he has all the imagination of a beached whale. I wanted *Natsiq* because I had designed our submarine to be smooth and fast like a seal. And it resembles a seal when it is swimming underwater: a sleek, tapered torpedo. I had decided that I could do far worse than copying Sedna, the Mother of the Sea's design.

During the final planning, I found out that Frank couldn't read or speak Inuktitut or any of our native languages. I had Carol and Kane work *Natsiq* into the paint design below *Nanook*. When evil Kootoo had asked, I'd simply said it was the submarine's name using the Inuktitut syllabary. As I was telling the truth, he detected nothing out of place.

After the tours and lunch, the first afternoon of the races is utter mayhem.

Twenty-six submarines get launched into the massive tank as fast as each team can clear their entry down the ramp of the dry dock. Hundreds of students, team advisors, and DTMB safety personnel are all kitted up in full scuba gear as we begin our testing. University of Virginia's submarine instantly sinks to the bottom of the tank. University of Sussex's sub won't sink at all, bobbing about like a cork.

As teams work on each of their individual issues, I'm glad to see that, with only minor adjustments to the ballast tanks, *Natsiq* floats well and holds its two-meter depth.

I wait until Carol and Kane are submerged with the submarine before speaking to Kootoo as nicely as I can. "Don't show off, Frank. We want to keep our abilities as a surprise. And I need to tune the drive. I've never seen it really work before."

He offers a sea walrus grunt before we both bite down on our regulators and ease underwater to float beside *Natsiq*.

Despite being an inlander—Fairbanks campus lies two hundred and fifty miles and a mountain range from the nearest ocean—Frank Kootoo has incredible endurance. Though we're much the same size, I was never able to match his power in the tests. *Natsiq* needs more finesse than power, but telling Kootoo that had not placed me in the cockpit. It is the one role he claimed for himself as our project manager. Now I'm left to worry how much of the glory he will take for himself over the next five days.

Most of the smaller submersibles place the human pilot face down. The design can be slimmer for a prone driver than a sitting one. This also places their feet by the rear propeller shortening the drivetrain and saving weight and complexity. Their faces are in a small bubble-window at the bow. But the position makes it very awkward to pedal.

The larger ones, typically with two pedaler-pilots, sit

upright, either side-by-side or in tandem. They make up for the longer-heavier drivetrain with more power.

I had spent hours balancing myself in different positions on sawhorses in our garage back home, measuring how much power I could apply for how long, to a set of bicycle pedals. Then I repeated the whole exercise in the pool, nearly drowning myself twice.

The recumbent cycling position won hands-down.

In *Natsiq* the driver sits comfortably, back braced against a mesh seat, and is able to see because the entire upper section is clear acrylic. And with my drivetrain, the point at which the power itself gets generated is irrelevant as half of the drive is at the bow and half at the stern. I sacrificed a few kilos of mass in exchange for an entirely new thrust system.

Most of the submarines use some form of a propeller. Fat blades like an outboard motor, thin blades like an airplane propeller, even a *hélice monopale* single-blade which solves numerous complex flow issues. A few use flapping mirage blades that wash back and forth like paired underwater wings. There is nothing here like my circular impellers.

Kootoo hands off his tanks to Kane, bites down on the regulator attached to the on-board air tank and slips into *Natsiq*. He is barely clamped in under the hatch when he takes off. It's a good thing I didn't use a traditional propeller or one of us might have been hurt.

He recklessly sweeps down the pool's length, scattering other teams. Safety inspectors begin to shout, to no effect as Kootoo is underwater and has left the rest of us far behind.

I'm glad that I didn't show him the real trick to gain speed. Even so, he's ruined most of my surprise.

Then, since we haven't had a chance yet to fine tune the systems, I can see him drifting off course and rising.

My shout spits out my regulator mouthpiece, and I have to surface as I choke out my rage. Kootoo surfaces just in time for me to see him ram the University of Sussex's sub broadside—which, after being stuck on the surface, now sinks abruptly.

3

My goal of hiding in my hotel room until the end of the apocalypse, or at least until after the races and Christmas, is foiled by Vlad before I even leave DTMB.

"No. The hiding is not good. You are not some seal and he is not a polar bear waiting to eat you."

"No, it only feels that way."

"Exactly!"

Vlad is right. If I sit in the room that Carol and I are sharing, I'll stew about Kootoo on the other side of the thin hotel wall.

Instead of spending an afternoon finally testing and tuning our entry, we spend it helping the University of Sussex fix theirs.

All of our submarines are *wet,* filled with water except for the stream of bubbles rising off the on-board scuba gear. They purposely aren't watertight. This is good because the University of Sussex's boat would never be truly tight again after Kootoo rammed it.

Kane, Carol, and I spent the rest of the afternoon helping them refit their sub. They almost rebuffed our offer.

But they calmed down when Kane spotted why they were having buoyancy issues—the flight over from the UK had expanded several air pockets in their lightweight honeycomb fiberglass, which hadn't collapsed on landing. A few judicious holes drilled, the honeycomb compressed, and then the holes patched had solved their excessive buoyancy issues. I also showed them a trick to gain ten percent more power by adding two springs to balance out drive lash and we ended up getting along.

While I was doing this, Kootoo had made several runs at me about the flaky buoyancy trim of *Natsiq. Why aren't you working on something important, like fixing our submarine instead of theirs, Ashoona?*

Do trolls have nine lives? I mean if my glare finally kills him, will he come back eight more times?

And now that I'm done helping fix Sussex's sub, he's after me again.

"Why aren't you staying to fix ours now that you've wasted all afternoon helping someone else?"

Before I can waste time explaining to evil-Kootoo that Day One is over and they're starting to chase us out of the building, Bethany the dog handler had strolled up with Tricky Gal. Her German Shepherd, having a good memory, has a snarl ready for Kootoo.

He opens his mouth, then shuts it very quickly when a male handler walks up with a massive Russian Bear Dog. The dog's head is even with Kootoo's gut and probably weighs more than he does even under all that fur.

"Get these stupid beasts—" is as far as Kootoo gets before the big dog unleashes a bark that echoes hard off the rounded ceiling and silences the entire length of the pool.

Kootoo stumbles away, plunging backward into the pool several feet below.

Of course *he* hasn't been hurt. But everyone is delayed because he breaks the arm of one of University of Warwick's swimmers who he landed on.

Carol and Kane are nowhere to be seen. Keeping out of target range, I suppose. The moment the day was declared done, they evaporated.

And I, now that the medics are gone...

"Yes," I looked at Vlad. "Get me out of here fast." Because I could guarantee that Kootoo would find some way to make everything my fault if he found me again.

As good as his word, Vlad had me out the door and into a taxi faster than I could catch my breath. Good thing the evening wasn't cold enough to zip my parka because he didn't leave me enough time for that.

"Thai or Irish?"

"Let's see. In Nome I have a choice of seafood, pizza, seafood, a couple of Chinese places, or seafood. Though there are some good food carts for the Iditarod finish line each year, mostly serving seafood or seafood." In fact, the farthest I've ever been from Nome was to Anchorage for scuba training.

"Meaning?"

"Meaning I have no idea from either one."

"That is meaning the Irish stew we get."

The driver nods and we're on our way.

"Ashoona, huh?" He asks when we settle in the restaurant.

The Irish Inn at Glen Echo has dark wood floors and tables. Twinkle lights and wreaths are tasteful in a way never seen in Nome. And even before I look at the menu, the rolled linen napkins on the white tablecloths tells me that this place is crazy way out of my budget. None of the other diners are dressed in student garb after a day of diving in a Navy boat basin.

Vlad doesn't miss my expression and insists that it's his treat. "You can buy us pizza tomorrow."

Like, of course, we're going to be sharing dinner tomorrow. I'm at a loss. But when I order a safe cheeseburger, he shakes his head so sadly that I tell him to order for me. He goes straight to one of the most expensive items, the Guinness Beef Stew, and a Banger Plate for himself. Maybe he'll hit himself on the head with it.

He also orders two of something called black-and-tans. When they come, I don't point out to the waiter that I'm not twenty-one yet. A Christmas baby, I will be in another seven days. And I'd still love some award from the ISR sitting under the tree—other than Most Reviled Team in History.

Besides, I'm intrigued, the light and dark beers float separately in the same glass, brown-black on top and pale below.

"Different specific gravities," Vlad explains.

I tip the glass slightly side-to-side to inspect the stability of the boundary-layer mixing. More stable than cream in coffee, but less than ice on the sea. Perhaps a slush-water boundary state, stable until disturbed.

"Watch as you drink it, too. The volume shift will change their ratios as you drink and it changes all the flavor. It begins heavy dark. Then more light as the layer of Bass Ale arriving from underneath."

My first taste is dark enough to chew. And only now do I realize that rescuing me probably wasn't Vlad's first priority. Was he thinking this is a date? I try to think of why I'm letting him *rescue* me so easily? That too isn't hard. He's like a sight of home in a blizzard. Until yesterday's flights, I had never been out of Alaska.

"Qarpik, huh?" I move the conversation back to where

he'd started it. It will let me talk about home. It doesn't take long to figure out that we aren't related, but that my grandparents and his go way back as friends and that we each have relatives who live near the other.

"Okay, I guess that means that we are fated to meet," Vlad announces as the food arrives.

"Sure, you and I grew up under two hundred miles apart. Yet I had to travel four thousand miles across North America..."

"And I must travel twenty thousand kilometers across Russia, Europe, and the Atlantic Ocean. So, yes, of course, it was fates." Vlad nods as if assuring me that it all makes sense.

"Are you sure it wasn't a *Qualupalik* that brought you here?"

Vlad laughed and it is the laugh of home. Not some great roar that might scare off game, but it came from deep inside. "Do you think that if the child-thieving mermaid had captured me, she would let me go so easily?"

"She must have had some reason. Maybe it is your Russian accent that gave her indigestion." Of course we're having the whole meal in Inuktitut, so his accent is of the Bering Sea Inuit, not Russia.

"Or maybe too pretty to keep."

Now it is my turn to laugh. He is. Handsome and funny.

And it is only when he kisses me outside the room that what he really meant sinks in—he meant me maybe being too pretty for *Qualupalik* to keep.

I know I'm pretty enough. I have my mother's curves and grandmother's straight fall of black hair. I'm fine featured for an Inuit. Boys are always attracted to my body.

But his kiss is only partly about that.

Vlad and I sat for hours past the bread pudding topped

with Baileys Irish Cream dessert, talking fluid viscosity, ramifications of how we each calculated the Froude number for our speed-length ratios, even thermal and pressure effects on composite versus acrylic surfaces.

I let the kiss melt me down like spring thaw, knowing we only have five days together. Four, one is already gone.

I'm past caring when I float into my room with Carol.

She and Kane are asleep under a blanket on the couch. Avoiding evil Kootoo. I always knew they were both smart. I turn off the TV quietly playing *White Christmas*—I hadn't realized they were Bing Crosby musicals kind of mushes— and crawl into bed.

Somehow, the disaster that reigned supreme for so much of the day no longer touches me.

4

THE FEELING LASTS PRECISELY TEN MINUTES AFTER I GET UP for Day Two.

"No sign of Frank," Kane announces after going to his own room for a quick change and shower.

I know what evil Kootoo has done. He's decided that he knows best and has worked through the night *improving* my poor innocent *Natsiq*. I should have made sure he left when the rest of us did rather than escaping while the medics were carting away the injured Warwick student. I should have talked to the security teams at DTMB to make sure that none of us would be allowed back into the building. Except they had already said that.

We trade grim looks.

Kootoo has done it before, and been wrong in so many ways.

Day Two will be spent undoing whatever he's done. If it's bad, we could well miss the maneuverability trials today, having already missed the shakedown opportunity.

Even Vlad's cheery wave from the bus that picks us up

does nothing to brighten the gloom. No snow in Potomac, Maryland. No White Christmas. And no merriness under the tree next week if we fail.

Vlad tries a hug when we unload at the Basin, but even that doesn't shake loose my own personal cloud.

The feeling is...*Qapalaqijuq*—whiteout.

I'm out on the ice. There is no snow, no sea, and the sky is hazed white, masking the sun. I can see for miles, except there's nothing to see. The disorienting, flat-light whiteout can send the most seasoned hunter walking in endless circles because the ice and the sky are a single color, a single surface. I can see for kilometers, but the light is so unrevealing that without the horizon I can't keep my balance.

Disaster in every direction I look.

Yet *Natsiq* is in her cradle precisely where we left her last night.

Her bow is still crumpled from ramming the University of Sussex's submarine.

All four of our wetsuits and tanks are lined up together. I check, Kootoo's is dry.

Kane and Carol work on the bow while I go through the rest of the systems. Nothing is out of order. Kootoo crashed so quickly that it isn't even worth topping up the on-board air tank.

In fact, inside an hour, *Natsiq* is ready and the only thing still unaccounted for is Frank Kootoo.

"You sure he wasn't in the room?"

Kane shakes his head and whispers. "Guy's a slob, but there wasn't a wrinkle on either bed."

"Maybe he got lucky?"

Carol shuddered. "Ick! Who would want to touch..." she

looked around quickly and lowered her voice further "...*that.*"

No one I could imagine.

"He's gotten way worse than when we started."

"I thought that was just me."

Carol shook her head. I wasn't sure how Carol and Kane had survived being on the same campus with him. I was hundreds of miles away for almost the entire project. Like Vlad, I was the team's design engineer—though his team had three.

By lunch, there is still no sign of Kootoo.

I consider calling the police or the hospital, but I don't want them to find him. I want to drive in the International Submarine Race. Doing it without him? Happy walrus-hunt dance.

We're bumped to the back of the queue because we're missing our registered sub driver.

We keep our silence, finally no longer able to meet each other's eyes. We fuss with *Natsiq* while waiting for the other shoe to drop.

But it doesn't.

Finally, we can't wait any longer and I enter the water as the primary driver. I change out the regulator in the sub for my own spare. I slip through the hatch, shedding my scuba tanks into Kane's care.

I exhale my held breath to clear the sub's regulator and then breathe in carefully. Only a few drips of water, my breathing settles quickly even if my heart rate doesn't.

Once I'm seated and belted in, they seal the hatch over my head. We take a moment to scan all directions, but the only person in view is the swimming ISR official ready to signal our start.

I finally look at Carol and Kane through the acrylic. I offer a thumbs-up and they both thump a fist on the hull for luck. They flutter their fins to swim aside and I'm floating free.

The official places three fingers into an open palm, asking about my air.

I hold up three fingers to indicate that I have three thousand psi on my gauge. Did Kootoo even breathe before he crashed? Maybe he really is an evil spirit who doesn't need air at all. Perhaps he is a *Qualupalik* come to steal *our* souls.

The official signals with an OK sign as a question which I return as a statement.

Then he points two index fingers ahead down the tank, one in the lead, telling me to go ahead and he'll follow.

I drive my right foot down.

In a pedal-powered wet sub, interior turbulence can be almost as big a problem as external. As I drive my right foot forward, special ducting circulates the excess water into the underside of my left pedal. This captures much of the right-foot energy. Rather than being a hindrance, I reuse it.

Meanwhile, the top of my left-foot water is driving water up into another duct which circulates the water downward. As my right foot bottoms out, the surge from the top of my left foot is driving against the bottom of my right. I augment this in turn as I drive down the left pedal.

Within three strokes, the pedal motion is very light, each foot doing half the work for the other—thirty-seven percent actually, but still very efficient. I will tire at least thirty-seven percent less than if I were pedaling in a chamber where the water could slosh at will.

In experiments I tried a two-foot drive like a rowing

machine, but couldn't smooth out the strokes from push to pull because of the fluid dynamics.

The push-me pull-you system works so smoothly that I'm up to the first marker before I'm ready. I lose time stopping my foot motion, reversing the gear linkage, taking two strokes to slow, stop again and shift to forward, before I can safely make the turn outside the pylon.

I won't make that mistake again.

So much harder than it had looked in simulations, I twist my way down the course. Evil Kootoo had far more practice time than I did, but I quickly reconcile the differences between the calculated handling, that has filled my head these last months, versus reality. My timing smooths out quickly, and I avoid the point-losing mistake of poor depth control. The last gate is mind-bogglingly difficult. I have to pass through a gate going forward, reverse *around* the gate, then pass through it backwards.

I will definitely make some changes to the steering controls before I try that again.

After I emerge, we three slide *Natsiq* back onto her cart, and roll her up the ramp to dry out. Everyone else is waiting on us to finish before the officials can announce the results. The three of us sit in our full dive gear and drip on anyone who comes close.

Four subs missed the final reverse maneuver entirely. They simply blew through the gate and thought they were done. Another fourteen were unable to complete the maneuver. I feel less awful about my initial blunder and the difficulties with my steering setup as they list the final eight from bottom to top.

"Third!" Carol screams in my ear. Kane picks me up in a bear hug and jiggles me up and down several times.

Then they announce second for *ÉTS*. Which means—

Vlad shoots me a big grin as his team erupts in cheers.

Okay, I'll have to hate him for a while, but I return the smile and add a thumbs-up to show that I won't hold it against him for too long.

5

VLAD INVITES US OUT, OUR WHOLE TEAM.

His team is going to mob a local pizzeria.

"It *is* your turn to do the buying," he winks.

"No way am I buying pizza for your entire team." Though after placing third I'm very ready to celebrate.

But there still no sign of Kootoo, evil or otherwise.

With our professor still sick in Alaska and Kootoo missing, the team responsibility has fallen to me.

I promise Vlad that we'll join them after I place a few calls. It takes a half hour; no news from any of the hospitals. Out of ideas, I notify the police.

We don't we get our pizza. I figure out all too quickly that we won't be getting much sleep either. The police discover that Kootoo has been lying to us about being twenty, he's actually seventeen—obnoxious kid genius. That makes him a missing minor, which escalates everything.

I've visited the Nome police station plenty of times. I had seriously crushed on one of the patrolman only two years my senior and quickly learned that, being the youngest on the staff, he had a lot of long quiet evenings manning the

29

desk. Other than drunk and disorderlies, not all that much happens in an isolated town of less than four thousand people. We never dared do much in the police station, but we'd sit and talk for hours while he ate my fresh-baked cookies.

We never talked like Vlad and I did last night, but he was so pretty—until he began dating Sue Renner—all blonde and skinny. After that I was done with him, though once I calmed down and got over the other version of being crushed, I never regretted those long cookie evenings.

In all that time, I never saw the inside of an interrogation room. In Potomac, Maryland I sure did. It's a dismal place: a gray table, chairs that squeak every time I shift my weight, which echoes off the concrete walls painted whiteout white.

They were very clear that we weren't being charged or under arrest. They did roust a public defender for us, but she never protested about a single question or answer. Though she took enough notes that I ended up more scared of her than the police.

The police were nice, but they kept us for hours asking details of Frank Kootoo's habits and ways. Where he'd been when we last saw him and where we'd been since. Soon the military police were involved at DTMB. Then I remembered the two dog handlers, and they were hauled out of bed as well.

We didn't detail his horribleness, but it was easy to state and have corroborated—maybe I've watched *CSI* too many times—that he was universally disliked. We then had to do our best to recall each person he had insulted or injured. It was a long list.

The kid from University of Warwick doesn't remember much other than the pain of fracturing his forearm across the sub's hull when Kootoo landed on him. He tries to shrug it off as an accident, which it was, but I can see how angry he is at having to sit on the race sidelines, too drugged to be of much use and definitely not able to swim with a cast. The shrug apparently punched through the painkillers.

I broke my arm in fourth grade gym class when I fell off the uneven parallel bars. I don't tell him that the itching begins when the painkillers wear off.

We plunge into bed just three hours before we have to wake up.

That Kane slides in with Carol didn't surprise me at all. Other than checking that Kootoo hadn't magically resurfaced, none of us want anything to do with his room.

"No sex while I'm sleeping in the same room as you two."

Carol and I took Kane's snore as an answer.

I barely have time to think of Vlad before we both collapse ourselves.

6

DAY THREE. PRESENTATION DAY STARTED OUT OKAY.

Innovation. I want the Innovation Award. Each sub team has been given twenty minutes to present what is special about their craft. I can't scribble notes fast enough.

A year ago I'd been a physics major, dreaming of getting a high school teaching job when I graduated to help finance a Master's degree that I had no idea what I'd do with. Maybe teach at University of Alaska, Fairbanks some day. No... Anchorage. I didn't want to be so far from the sea. Nome was strictly a remote-access campus, so not an option.

Then my professor had started talking about a senior project. *Design something amazing, Malee. You have the mind for it.*

Total news to me. I decided to design a submarine. I understood boats—sixteen-foot aluminum ones with an outboard engine used for hunting walrus each spring. We weren't a whaling family, but their boats were little different except for the harpoon.

I still don't know quite how I found the ISR but once I did I couldn't think of anything even half as cool. My professor found me a team at Fairbanks, and we were, literally, off to the races.

Still, it had simply been my senior project, which I was plenty competitive about because it's the sort of person I am. That all changed when I saw the video invitation to this year's races. When former ISR competitor Megan McArthur greeted us from the International Space Station and said she'd launched herself from the ISR to become a NASA scientist and pilot, I knew I had a dream.

One I hadn't even told Vlad, though it had occupied so much of my thoughts for nine months now.

McArthur said that her success came from pursuing something she loved with all her heart.

And I loved my design, but especially my drivetrain innovation.

We were presenting alphabetically, which put me in the middle of the pack. University comes late in the alphabet but Alaska was the first of the many universities represented at ISR.

The *Natsiq* was going to be the first one after lunch.

"You aren't afraid of your teammate showing up and having of all the glory?" Vlad sat down across the table from me.

Carol and Kane had taken sandwiches and wandered off somewhere.

"Not until you said that, no." Now I was. That would be so evil-Kootoo of him because he'd get twice the attention than if he'd merely tried to grab the glory as I'd expected. Hiding out until we were so worried about him that I was thinking far less of his horriblity and more of his skills as a project manager. We might be a dysfunctional team, but under his control we had built a wonderful craft with the smallest team here.

The Grenoble INP Institut d'ingénierie eleven-person team had presented early this morning. I had three pages of notes from their twenty-minute presentation. Their drive was nothing special, but they were almost sure to win Smooth Operator because of their immaculate coordination, and Team Spirit for their can-do attitude. Everybody liked their team, who were always helping out anyone who was struggling. And they were a hot contender for Overall Design because while they weren't the strongest, they had the fewest weaknesses. They'd really pulled it together as a team at every level.

"Maybe his ghosting will come to haunt you?" Vlad wiggled his fingers like an invading fog. "And maybe I will humble you completely in the speed trials."

"Only if you drag it down the pool with one of the Navy's high-speed testing carriages." The Grenoble two-person craft is actually a very fast boat. They had decided on a twin-hull configuration using dual propellers, one driven by each pedaler. No steering mechanism, instead they worked as a team and varied their pedaling rates to steer. Simplification had provided lightweight drivetrains and no steering meant fewer moving parts. Their long-blade props stuck out past the sub's turbulence so that they were always biting clear water.

And their depth control was incredible in its simplicity. They had a selectable valve for whatever pressure depth they wished to maintain. It controlled the release of air coming from the diving regulators that had accumulated in the cabin. Brilliantly simple.

"You did the depth regulator." I finally connect that fact to the focus of Vlad's interests over our one dinner together.

He bowed over his lunch tray.

"That was...elegant."

Vlad slapped a hand to his chest as if overcome. "The few. The proud."

"The Marines."

"What?" He squinted at me.

"The United States Marines. That's their recruiting slogan. I didn't know they were recruiting Russians who study in France."

Vlad scratched his head. "I'm not a fighter."

"A lover then." And the heat slammed to my face so that it burned. I had *not* just said that. We'd kissed once. That's all. Yet he'd occupied almost as much of my thoughts as *Natsiq* and Kootoo had in the last thirty hours since he'd gone missing.

I was trying to figure some way out of the flirt-hole I had just cut through the ice, without jumping in to become polar bear bait. I wasn't coming up with anything as my cheeks continued to burn.

Vlad's smile was big and growing bigger by the second.

Then something cold pressed up against my neck and I yelped as Vlad laughed.

"Sorry, he does that," a man's voice spoke behind me.

When I twisted in my seat, I was nose-to-nose with the Great Russian Bear Dog. He licked my face.

"You must be washing that before I try kissing you again," Vlad managed through a laugh.

"He never does that," the handler called for the big dog to heel. "He must like you. Don't tell my wife, she'll be jealous." The dog plomped onto his butt and was still at eye-to-eye level.

"At least he's not a polar bear."

"Wrong color," Vlad remarked.

I ignore him. I understand his growing smile now, he'd seen the dog coming.

"Could you come with us?" The handler isn't looking amused, which has the benefit of cutting off Vlad's laugh.

When I follow him and his monstrous dog, I can't help staring at the white *Police* printed in big block letters across the back of his vest. I jump when Vlad takes my hand, but I decide that I appreciate the moral support.

"Is she in trouble?"

"No, sir. Not that I know of."

I hadn't even thought of that.

He leads us down the length of the pool, past the wave generator, which can create model-sized hurricane force turbulence in the tank when testing surface ships. We take a left around the broad square tank used for testing turn-maneuverability. There is a cluster of people gathered at the far end of the pool.

A *lot* of them have Police vests. The other patrol dog is there as well. As are Carol and Kane.

"What's going on?"

But the answer is heaved onto the side of the pool as I watch. It's the padded slip-cover Carol had made for *Natsiq* to protect it during shipping from Alaska. The color of the Alaskan Sea, it was nearly invisible in a shadowed corner of the presently unused tank. At only five feet deep, the turning tank isn't of much use for submarine testing, so no one had come by here.

On the concrete at the edge of the pool, the shipping cover looks like a beached blue seal.

Carol has turned her face into Kane's shoulder.

Vlad's strong hand is all that's sustaining my knees at the moment, but I can't look away.

They unzip the cover.

I'd know that face anywhere, it's been in enough of my nightmares.

"That's Frank Kootoo." And now I do turn to hide my face in Vlad's shoulder.

He looks so...dead. Dead and still angry about it.

Even though he's gone, I don't want to do a happy-walrus-hunt dance at all.

7

THE DAY BLURRED ON ME.

"Valentin," the handler patted the Great Russian Bear Dog's head, "triggered on his scent here at the poolside. But it was so tentative that I didn't pick up on it. Sorry, boy. I missed my cue," he apologized to the dog.

A lot more questions, so I miss most of the other presentations. But I insist that I'm okay to do ours. I've had so many questions about our peculiar looking setup that I told everyone to wait for the presentation.

Of course, with all the police's questions, once again we're bumped to the end of the day. Not that I'm complaining. It has taken me all afternoon to get around the lump in my throat.

I won't miss Frank Kootoo for a second. But he's dead so I should. That I don't is messing with my head.

I test my feelings like a sore tooth. I still feel worse about my very distant Uncle Natak who was killed by that polar bear three years ago than I do about Frank Kootoo.

"I initially thought of my drive system from watching a movie called *The Core.*" I start the talk in the big auditorium that is standing-room only with all of the teams and military observers. And several police keeping an eye on the crowd, which I try to ignore.

The movie reference earns me a round of unexpected laughter, including Vlad's. He sat in the front row to cheer me on. What is surprising is how much he steadies my nerves. The biggest group I've ever presented to before was my professor and the three members of my team.

The Core is a ridiculous movie scientifically. It's about an experiment that goes wrong and stops the Earth's spinning core. A team of scientists create a boring-machine ship able to drill all the way down through the crust and mantle, where they fire off a whole series of nuclear explosions to restart the core—which saves the world.

But we're all a bunch of science nerds here, so of course we've watched every science fiction movie that's science-based instead of being a monster hunt—and a lot of those if they did a decent job on the ship design and science.

"I noticed that their ship had paired, counterrotating impellers to drive the ship forward. The counterrotation is necessary so that it doesn't simply make the ship spin the other direction. But I was deeply bothered by their close coupling as the flow dynamics of the molten lava would become highly turbulated by the first set of blades, making the second set useless."

Now everyone who has seen the film is nodding their heads or squinting into the distance as they try to remember it. I show a ten-second clip of the launch where the impellers are very clear. More nods.

"It took me three months of modeling to come up with the flow design for *Natsiq.*" I put a detailed image of the computed fluid dynamics of our submarine's drive up on the screen.

I try not to cringe that I'm no longer using Kootoo's *Nanook* name. Am I dishonoring the dead, even though it has always been *Natsiq* in my head? I forge on before that knot can wrap around my throat once more like a scarf wound too tightly and become frozen in place.

"Our forward impeller circles the outside of the boat at one-third of the way along the boat's length. I engineered the blade shape, and added an air bubble layer like the USS *Albatross* submarine to create a smooth flow past the forward impeller." I show a video of a smooth sheaf of air bubbles releasing directly behind the first impeller. "By disconnecting the water friction from the hull's surface, I was able to re-smooth the hydrodynamic flow for the aft impeller as well as significantly reduce drag."

There's a moment of silence and then a small round of applause. This has happened in a few of the other team's presentations and it's exciting that *Natsiq's* unique drive is getting that kind of spontaneous reaction.

I get another round of applause after detailing my pedal-enhancing ductwork.

"Steering is achieved primarily by applying a differential spin rate between the two counterrotating impellers to bank the craft, and then powering straight using the dive planes to control correction to the new course. I sacrificed three percent of the impeller's performance by making them symmetrical fore and aft. Because of this, it is equally efficient and fast in both forward or reverse. Though it needs a rearview mirror," I remind myself out loud.

Which earns me an unexpected laugh and an unprecedented third round of applause.

I include several shots of Carol and Kane machining the drive that I had designed.

And then I know what I have to do.

I put up the last image, the shot of the four of us and our professor gathered together around *Natsiq* at the U of A Fairbanks twenty-five-yard Patty Pool.

"Whatever we may each think of him," not my most tactful, "we could never have achieved this without the project coordination provided by Frank Kootoo. May we have a moment of silence for him."

And I let the last minute of my presentation run out in a grinding silence. It not only precludes any of the summation applause that the other teams received, but also proves incredibly awkward to break.

But in the silence I figured something out—someone in the room is a murderer.

8

Frank Kooto's evil is far from over. Not that I'm thinking ill of the dead or anything.

Day Four is the day for the speed tests. The pool is nine hundred meters long, just under a thousand yards. Our submarines mostly run around five to six knots. Six knots means sustaining an all-out sprint for over four-and-a-half full minutes. If I can sustain seven knots, that saves me forty seconds, and sets a world record. The unimaginable eight knots? That would require only three minutes and twenty-five seconds of flat-out exertion. Maybe.

We never had a chance to test *Natsiq's* full speed because we ran out of pool too fast in Alaska. Now we were jumping from a twenty-five yard pool to a thousand. It's the great unknown for most of the teams and no one has been bragging.

I understand why Frank rushed off that first morning he was in the sub; we were all dying to see what it could do. And now I was thinking of him by his first name. ICK! And using the word *dying* in the same sentence. Double ick!

Overnight we learned that there was no family to

contact, just an orphanage. And he'd been so unpopular in his freshman year that they'd given him a single dorm room almost immediately.

But being dead didn't stop him from continuing to make all of our lives awful. The police have a murder on their hands, so we're being guarded.

"Guarded or corralled?" Vlad of course finds a way to make everything funny.

Except his question isn't. "No escaping your foul crimes, Vlad." I try to keep it light as well.

"Hey, I have perfect alibi, I was out to dinner with you."

"Maybe they think we did it together." They've definitely been asking both of us a lot of questions. Well, me, and then pulling in Vlad because we're each other's alibi. "Or maybe you did it after kissing me goodnight at my room?"

"You know, at our normal latitude, I could be kissing you for nineteen hours in the same night."

"In December," I answer, though I wouldn't mind trying that. And it was a *great* subject change. "Of course, you could only do it for two-and-a-half hours in mid-summer."

"We could switch to daylight kissing in summer."

I laugh at the tease.

Of course, after the kiss is where our alibis collapse. Vlad had drawn the single room due to an uneven number of team members. And Carol and Kane were fast asleep when I slipped into my own room.

The police now know that Frank died that first night by analyzing the food in his stomach (*Ew!*): that first lunch and how much it was digested (*Double Ew!*). But they can't pin down an exact time.

"I don't think I was helping our case last night." Unable to sleep after the discovery of Kootoo's body and our presentation, I had wandered down the hall to Vlad's room.

My knock was little more than a scrape of knuckles on wood, but he answered almost immediately. He'd taken one look at my face and pulled me in.

I was so dazed that until that moment I hadn't imagined he would probably assume I wanted sex.

Vlad was smarter than that. We curled up in his bed together, and he let me sleep on his shoulder, which was exactly what I'd needed. I had slipped away to shower before he woke.

Despite having slept together, we were still at one kiss, at least as far as Vlad knew. I had left him with a kiss of thanks while he slept. It was nice to be held when I was one of the likely suspects for someone's murder.

9

SPEED TRIAL DAY STARTED EXACTLY AS THE LAST SEVERAL HAD
—talking about Frank Kootoo.

The police showed me footage of him from the night he died. I'd brought along Carol and Kane. Vlad had brought himself and I wasn't complaining.

They fast-scrolled through footage of security sweeping the building and all of us trailing out. Ten minutes later by the timer in the corner, Frank had emerged from some hiding place. A security camera had caught him sitting and staring at *Natsiq*—for hours.

Just staring. Like he was thinking incredibly hard about something.

Not working on fixing the damage, which was just as well, he wasn't much of a mechanic. Just thinking.

"He sat there for three hours barely moving. Do you have any idea what he might have been thinking?"

I looked at Carol and Kane, but we all shook our heads.

How little did we know about our fellow team member? We hadn't known he was seventeen, or an orphan. None of it.

"He kept himself to himself," I finally answered for the others.

"We found out that you three were the ones he was closest to, on campus or off."

Vlad handed me some tissues and waved for me to mop my face. I did, but it didn't stop the tears.

"After three hours he stood…"

He gave the camera so foul a grimace that it should have cracked the glass. Then he did something that made no sense. He bent down and picked up *Natsiq's* ocean-blue shipping cover—before walking out of the frame.

"He walked away from the direction of the exit and didn't appear on any camera again. He must have spotted and avoided all the cameras. We also found this on his phone." The policeman put up a short message on the screen.

> *I could never be as good as you.*
> *Not that I ever tried before this project.*
> *Thanks for believing in me, Malee.*

"What?" I couldn't make any sense of the words. "It sounds like a suicide note. But he was murdered."

The officer shook his head. "He gathered forty pounds of diving weights, tucked them in the bag at the edge of the pool. He appears to have zipped himself in, then rolled off the edge and into the water."

"But…why?" Vlad asked. The three of us were past speech.

The officer put up one last image.

It was an autopsy report, with one section highlighted.

Inoperable brain tumor.

Hard-pressed against amygdala,
center for aggression and fear responses.

Vlad held me tightly as he asked the final question, "He knew?"

The policeman nodded. "The same problem made Charles Whitman climb the University of Texas tower in Austin in 1966. He gunned down eighteen and wounded thirty more in an hour-and-a-half shooting spree. Frank Kootoo knew this, we found it prominently marked on his laptop. Apparently Mr. Kootoo didn't want to do that. Apparently especially not to you."

The four of us huddled together long after the policemen were gone.

10

──────────

"ARE YOU SURE YOU DON'T WANT ME TO DRIVE FOR YOU?"

I'd spent much of Speed Trial Day crying. So much so that they'd finally sedated me. Not enough to take me to the hospital for observation, but not good.

Vlad had taken me to his room, and I'd spent the night clinging to him whenever the drug didn't keep me under.

The last day was Awards Day, but they'd offered our team a single time trial run early this morning.

"No Vlad," I gave him a kiss. "No, the Nanooks started this and for better or worse, we'll finish it."

He'd made sure I'd eaten and done a workout to clear the last of the drugs from my system. My biggest regret was that we'd had two nights together—and I'd been an utter wreck for both of them.

"You're the best." And I ducked under the water before he could reply.

Carol and Kane helped me lock in.

The ISR official began the signals ritual.

I hadn't ever liked Frank Kootoo, but now I at least understood him a bit. He'd fought against his own nature—

51

driven mostly mad by that brain tumor—until he'd decided that the world was better off without him.

The real surprise was that he also thought the world was better off *because* of me.

Well, I was going to prove that he was right—for him.

The official gave me the Go signal.

And boy did I go.

11

"AND THE TEAM SPIRIT AWARD GOES TO," THE ISR OFFICIAL opened his envelope, "Grenoble INP Institut d'ingénierie. His team unanimously decided that the thousand-dollar scholarship award goes to team captain Vlad Qarpik."

His team tackled him and hoisted him in the air, almost dropping him half a dozen times before they settled. Once he was on solid ground again, his gaze sought me out.

I realized that it wasn't only me he was wonderful to. He'd treated his people so well that I hadn't even known he was captain until this moment. As sorry as I felt for Frank, I wanted a team like Vlad's.

Again I was doing the crazy crying thing. I'd cried more in five days than in as many years. I didn't have to think about why this time. Tomorrow morning we had a flight back to Alaska. Tonight Vlad Qarpik had a redeye flight back to France. Not quite the antipodes of Nome, which lay where the South Atlantic ran into Antarctica, but close enough.

Awards, honorable mentions, and scholarships were

53

announced and the mood was festive. I did my best to shake it off and leave the pain inside.

Would Frank have felt the joy? *Could* he have?

I'd never know, so I'd better figure out how to live with it. Curiously, I felt as if I was living for two of us now. Excelling was no longer enough. Astronaut Megan McArthur had shown me the possible, and now it was up to me and me alone to do it.

Carol and Kane wrapped me in a crushing hug.

"What?"

"Speed. We got speed!"

I'd never heard the final numbers. Seven-point-seven knots. We'd broken the world speed record by over a mile per hour.

I dragged both of them up to the podium with me. I remembered to thank my grandparents, my professor, had to double back to thank my parents, Frank Kootoo (who deserved it evil or not), and finally, "The two best mechanics I've ever met!" And I held up both their hands in mine as they blushed fiercely.

The Innovation Award I accepted on my own, with a different kind of tears running down my face. I really had done something incredible. That is definitely going under my Christmas tree this year.

When Overall Design went to Vlad's team, I couldn't have been happier for him.

12

"WE LIVE ONLY TWO HUNDRED MILES APART," IT FELT LIKE A wail on my part. While it was true, his life was no longer in his Chukchi Peninsula village. It was in France.

Good thing I'd gotten Vlad well away from the others as they finished packing his submarine for shipping or I'd be making a major spectacle of myself. Carol and Kane had scrounged a new shipping bag to replace the one Frank had died in.

How long would Frank dog my footsteps? Years? A lifetime?

I better make his memory a friend if he's going to hang on like that. But I wasn't feeling very triumphant at the moment. In another hour Vlad would be gone and, no matter how stupid, it felt like a piece of me would be as lost as poor Frank the moment Vlad was gone.

That piece of me would be out walking circles in the *qapalaqijuq* with Frank, on the white ice under the white sky until we had no direction, no path, no hope.

"We could live closer," Vlad had that smile of his that said the solution was so simple if only I could figure it out.

Even the possibility of a solution gave me enough hope to spar with him.

"Where, the Diomede Islands?" The pair of American and Russian islands were four kilometers apart in the middle of the Bering Sea.

He laughed that rich, quiet laugh of home. "No, you goofball. Didn't you hear, Malee Ashoona?"

"Hear what?"

He rested his hands on both my shoulders to make me focus on him. "Your drive design blew everyone away. Every grad school in the competition would offer you a full-ride ticket."

How had I missed all that? Did that... "Including the Grenoble engineering program?"

"I already asked. How would you like to come live with me in France and design submarines?"

Vlad watches me closely for a long moment but he must see the answer in my eyes, because he leans in and kisses me with that wonderful smile of his.

"One condition," I manage to whisper over the beating of my heart after his powerhouse kiss. "How do you feel about space?"

Vlad leans back to look at the ceiling of the DTMB pool tunnel. But I know that he too is seeing the International Space Station and recalling Megan McArthur's invitation video.

"I am thinking..."

He looks back down at me, but his smile hasn't diminished at all. I know his answer and lay my head on his shoulder. With Vlad's beacon of hope I'll never be lost out in the winter whiteout again.

"First submariners on Mars?" he whispers into my hair.

I don't need to answer, I know he can feel my silent laugh. It's the best Christmas present ever.

———

If you enjoyed this book,
please consider leaving a review.
They really help.

Keep reading for an exciting excerpt from:
White House Protection Force #1: *Off the Leash*

AFTERWORD

For further information on the FURE's International Submarine Races: https://internationalsubmarineraces.org/

To watch the ISR 17 greeting from Astronaut Megan McArthur: https://youtu.be/njm7KguZ9oQ

My apologies for moving the ISR competition from June to December for the sake of the story.

OFF THE LEASH (EXCERPT)

IF YOU ENJOYED THAT, YOU'LL LOVE THE
NOVELS!

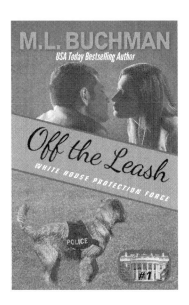

OFF THE LEASH (EXCERPT)

"You're joking."

"Nope. That's his name. And he's yours now."

Sergeant Linda Hamlin wondered quite what it would take to wipe that smile off Lieutenant Jurgen's face. A 120mm round from an M1A1 Abrams Main Battle Tank came to mind.

The kennel master of the US Secret Service's Canine Team was clearly a misogynistic jerk from the top of his polished head to the bottoms of his equally polished boots. She wondered if the shoelaces were polished as well.

Then she looked over at the poor dog sitting hopefully on the concrete kennel floor. His stall had a dog bed three times his size and a water bowl deep enough for him to bathe in. No toys, because toys always came from the handler as a reward. He offered her a sad sigh and a liquid doggy gaze. The kennel even smelled wrong, more of sanitizer than dog. The walls seemed to echo with each bark down the long line of kennels housing the candidate hopefuls for the next addition to the Secret Service's team.

Thor—really?—was a brindle-colored mutt, part who-knew and part no-one-cared. He looked like a cross between an oversized, long-haired schnauzer and a dust mop that someone had spilled dark gray paint on. After mixing in streaks of tawny brown, they'd left one white paw just to make him all the more laughable.

And of course Lieutenant Jerk Jurgen would assign Thor to the first woman on the USSS K-9 team.

Unable to resist, she leaned over far enough to scruff the dog's ears. He was the physical opposite of the sleek and powerful Malinois MWDs—military war dogs—that she'd been handling for the 75th Rangers for the last five years. They twitched with eagerness and nerves. A good MWD was seventy pounds of pure drive—every damn second of the day. If the mild-mannered Thor weighed thirty pounds, she'd be surprised. And he looked like a little girl's best friend who should have a pink bow on his collar.

Jurgen was clearly ex-Marine and would have no respect for the Army. Of course, having been in the Army's Special Operations Forces, she knew better than to respect a Marine.

"We won't let any old swabbie bother us, will we?"

Jurgen snarled—definitely Marine Corps. Swabbie was slang for a Navy sailor and a Marine always took offense at being lumped in with them no matter how much they belonged. Of course the swabbies took offense at having the Marines lumped with *them.* Too bad there weren't any Navy around so that she could get two for the price of one. Jurgen wouldn't be her boss, so appeasing him wasn't high on her to-do list.

At least she wouldn't need any of the protective bite gear working with Thor. With his stature, he was an explosives detection dog without also being an attack one.

"Where was he trained?" She stood back up to face the beast.

"Private outfit in Montana—some place called Henderson's Ranch. Didn't make their MWD program," his scoff said exactly what he thought the likelihood of any dog outfit in Montana being worthwhile. "They wanted us to try the little runt out."

She'd never heard of a training program in Montana. MWDs all came out of Lackland Air Force Base training. The Secret Service mostly trained their own and they all came from Vohne Liche Kennels in Indiana. Unless... Special Operations Forces dogs were trained by private contractors. She'd worked beside a Delta Force dog for a single month—he'd been incredible.

"Is he trained in English or German?" Most American MWDs were trained in German so that there was no confusion in case a command word happened to be part of a spoken sentence. It also made it harder for any random person on the battlefield to shout something that would confuse the dog.

"German according to his paperwork, but he won't listen to me much in either language."

Might as well give the diminutive Thor a few basic tests. A snap of her fingers and a slap on her thigh had the dog dropping into a smart "heel" position. No need to call out *Fuss—by my foot.*

"*Pass auf!*" Guard! She made a pistol with her thumb and forefinger and aimed it at Jurgen as she grabbed her forearm with her other hand—the military hand sign for enemy.

The little dog snarled at Jurgen sharply enough to have him backing out of the kennel. "Goddamn it!"

"*Ruhig.*" Quiet. Thor maintained his fierce posture but dropped the snarl.

"*Gute Hund.*" *Good dog,* Linda countered the command.

Thor looked up at her and wagged his tail happily. She tossed him a doggie treat, which he caught midair and crunched happily.

She didn't bother looking up at Jurgen as she knelt once more to check over the little dog. His scruffy fur was so soft that it tickled. Good strength in the jaw, enough to show he'd had bite training despite his size—perfect if she ever needed to take down a three-foot-tall terrorist. Legs said he was a jumper.

"Take your time, Hamlin. I've got nothing else to do with the rest of my goddamn day except babysit you and this mutt."

"Is the course set?"

"Sure. Take him out," Jurgen's snarl sounded almost as nasty as Thor's before he stalked off.

She stood and slapped a hand on her opposite shoulder.

Thor sprang aloft as if he was attached to springs and she caught him easily. He'd cleared well over double his own height. Definitely trained...and far easier to catch than seventy pounds of hyperactive Malinois.

She plopped him back down on the ground. On lead or off? She'd give him the benefit of the doubt and try off first to see what happened.

Linda zipped up her brand-new USSS jacket against the cold and led the way out of the kennel into the hard sunlight of the January morning. Snow had brushed the higher hills around the USSS James J. Rowley Training Center—which this close to Washington, DC, wasn't saying much—but was melting quickly. Scents wouldn't carry as well on the cool air, making it more of a challenge for Thor to locate the explosives. She didn't know where they were either. The course was a test for handler as well as dog.

Jurgen would be up in the observer turret looking for any excuse to mark down his newest team. Perhaps teasing him about being just a Marine hadn't been her best tactical choice. She sighed. At least she was consistent—she'd always been good at finding ways to piss people off before she could stop herself and consider the wisdom of doing so.

This test was the culmination of a crazy three months, so she'd forgive herself this time—something she also wasn't very good at.

In October she'd been out of the Army and unsure what to do next. Tucked in the packet with her DD 214 honorable discharge form had been a flyer on career opportunities with the US Secret Service dog team: *Be all your dog can be!* No one else being released from Fort Benning that day had received any kind of a job flyer at all that she'd seen, so she kept quiet about it.

She had to pass through DC on her way back to Vermont—her parent's place. Burlington would work for, honestly, not very long at all, but she lacked anywhere else to go after a decade of service. So, she'd stopped off in DC to see what was up with that job flyer. Five interviews and three months to complete a standard six-month training course later—which was mostly a cakewalk after fighting with the US Rangers—she was on-board and this chill January day was her first chance with a dog. First chance to prove that she still had it. First chance to prove that she hadn't made a mistake in deciding that she'd seen enough bloodshed and war zones for one lifetime and leaving the Army.

The Start Here sign made it obvious where to begin, but she didn't dare hesitate to take in her surroundings past a quick glimpse. Jurgen's score would count a great deal toward where she and Thor were assigned in the future.

Mostly likely on some field prep team, clearing the way for presidential visits.

As usual, hindsight informed her that harassing the lieutenant hadn't been an optimal strategy. A hindsight that had served her equally poorly with regular Army commanders before she'd finally hooked up with the Rangers—kowtowing to officers had never been one of her strengths.

Thankfully, the Special Operations Forces hadn't given a damn about anything except performance and *that* she could always deliver, since the day she'd been named the team captain for both soccer and volleyball. She was never popular, but both teams had made all-state her last two years in school.

The canine training course at James J. Rowley was a two-acre lot. A hard-packed path of tramped-down dirt led through the brown grass. It followed a predictable pattern from the gate to a junker car, over to tool shed, then a truck, and so on into a compressed version of an intersection in a small town. Beyond it ran an urban street of gray clapboard two- and three-story buildings and an eight-story office tower, all without windows. Clearly a playground for Secret Service training teams.

Her target was the town, so she blocked the city street out of her mind. Focus on the problem: two roads, twenty storefronts, six houses, vehicles, pedestrians.

It might look normal...normalish with its missing windows and no movement. It would be anything but. Stocked with fake IEDs, a bombmaker's stash, suicide cars, weapons caches, and dozens of other traps, all waiting for her and Thor to find. He had to be sensitive to hundreds of scents and it was her job to guide him so that he didn't miss the opportunity to find and evaluate each one.

There would be easy scents, from fertilizer and diesel fuel used so destructively in the 1995 Oklahoma City bombing, to almost as obvious TNT to the very difficult to detect C-4 plastic explosive.

Mannequins on the street carried grocery bags and briefcases. Some held fresh meat, a powerful smell demanding any dog's attention, but would count as a false lead if they went for it. On the job, an explosives detection dog wasn't supposed to care about anything except explosives. Other mannequins were wrapped in suicide vests loaded with Semtex or wearing knapsacks filled with package bombs made from Russian PVV-5A.

She spotted Jurgen stepping into a glassed-in observer turret atop the corner drugstore. Someone else was already there and watching.

She looked down once more at the ridiculous little dog and could only hope for the best.

"Thor?"

He looked up at her.

She pointed to the left, away from the beaten path.

"*Such!*" *Find.*

Thor sniffed left, then right. Then he headed forward quickly in the direction she pointed.

————

CLIVE ANDREWS SAT IN THE SECOND-STORY WINDOW AT THE corner of Main and First, the only two streets in town. Downstairs was a drugstore all rigged to explode, except there were no triggers and there was barely enough explosive to blow up a candy box.

Not that he'd know, but that's what Lieutenant Jurgen had promised him.

It didn't really matter if it was rigged to blow for real, because when Miss Watson—never Ms. or Mrs.—asked for a "favor," you did it. At least he did. Actually, he had yet to meet anyone else who knew her. Not that he'd asked around. She wasn't the sort of person one talked about with strangers, or even close friends. He'd bet even if they did, it would be in whispers. That's just what she was like.

So he'd traveled across town from the White House and into Maryland on a cold winter's morning, barely past a sunrise that did nothing to warm the day. Now he sat in an unheated glass icebox and watched a new officer run a test course he didn't begin to understand. Lieutenant Jurgen settled in beside him at a console with feeds from a dozen cameras and banks of switches.

While waiting, Clive had been fooling around with a sketch on a small pad of paper. The next State Dinner was in seven days. President Zachary Taylor had invited the leaders of Vietnam, Japan, and the Philippines to the White House for discussions about some Chinese islands. Or something like that, Clive hadn't really been paying attention to the details past the attendee list.

Instead, he was contemplating the dessert for such a dinner that would surprise, perhaps delight, as well as being an icebreaker for future discussions. Being the chocolatier for the White House was the most exciting job he'd ever had. Every challenge was fresh and new, like the first strawberry of each year.

This one would be elegant. January was a little early, it would be better if it was spring, but that wasn't crucial. A large half-egg shape of paper-thin white chocolate filled with a mousse—white chocolate? No, nor a dark chocolate. Instead, a milk chocolate mousse but rich with flavor, perhaps bourbon. Then mold the dark chocolate to top it with a filigree bird, wings spread in half flight, ready to soar upward. A crane perhaps? He made a note to check with the protocol office to make sure that he wouldn't be offending some leader without knowing it.

"Never underestimate the power of a good dessert," he mumbled one of Jacques Torres' favorite admonitions. This was going to work very nicely.

"What's that?" Jurgen grunted out without looking up.

"Just talking to myself."

Which earned him a dismissive grunt, as if he was unworthy of the agent's attention. It wouldn't surprise him.

———

Keep reading now!
Available at fine retailers everywhere.
Off the Leash

ABOUT THE AUTHOR

USA Today and Amazon #1 Bestseller M. L. "Matt" Buchman began writing on a flight from Japan to ride his bicycle across the Australian Outback. Just part of a solo around-the-world trip that ultimately launched his writing career.

From the very beginning, his powerful female heroines insisted on putting character first, *then* a great adventure. He's since written over 70 action-adventure thrillers and military romantic suspense novels. And just for the fun of it: 100 short stories, and a fast-growing pile of read-by-author audiobooks.

Booklist says: "3X Top 10 of the Year." PW says: "Tom Clancy fans open to a strong female lead will clamor for more." His fans say: "I want more now...of everything." That his characters are even more insistent than his fans is a hoot.

As a 30-year project manager with a geophysics degree who has designed and built houses, flown and jumped out of planes, and solo-sailed a 50' ketch, he is awed by what is possible. More at: www.mlbuchman.com.

Other works by M. L. Buchman: (* - also in audio)

Action-Adventure Thrillers

Dead Chef
One Chef!
Two Chef!

Miranda Chase
Drone*
Thunderbolt*
Condor*
Ghostrider*
Raider*
Chinook*
Havoc*
White Top*
Start the Chase*

Science Fiction / Fantasy

Deities Anonymous
Cookbook from Hell: Reheated
Saviors 101

Single Titles
Monk's Maze
the Me and Elsie Chronicles

Contemporary Romance

Eagle Cove
Return to Eagle Cove
Recipe for Eagle Cove
Longing for Eagle Cove
Keepsake for Eagle Cove

Love Abroad
Heart of the Cotswolds: England
Path of Love: Cinque Terre, Italy

Where Dreams
Where Dreams are Born
Where Dreams Reside
Where Dreams Are of Christmas*
Where Dreams Unfold
Where Dreams Are Written
Where Dreams Continue

Non-Fiction

Strategies for Success
Managing Your Inner Artist/Writer
Estate Planning for Authors*
Character Voice
Narrate and Record Your Own
Audiobook*

Short Story Series by M. L. Buchman:

Action-Adventure Thrillers

Dead Chef

Miranda Chase Origin Stories

Romantic Suspense

Antarctic Ice Fliers

US Coast Guard

Contemporary Romance

Eagle Cove

Other

Deities Anonymous (fantasy)

Single Titles

The Emily Beale Universe
(military romantic suspense)

The Night Stalkers
MAIN FLIGHT
The Night Is Mine
I Own the Dawn
Wait Until Dark
Take Over at Midnight
Light Up the Night
Bring On the Dusk
By Break of Day
Target of the Heart
Target Lock on Love
Target of Mine
Target of One's Own
NIGHT STALKERS HOLIDAYS
Daniel's Christmas*
Frank's Independence Day*
Peter's Christmas*
Christmas at Steel Beach
Zachary's Christmas*
Roy's Independence Day*
Damien's Christmas*
Christmas at Peleliu Cove

Henderson's Ranch
Nathan's Big Sky*
Big Sky, Loyal Heart*
Big Sky Dog Whisperer*
Tales of Henderson's Ranch*

Shadow Force: Psi
At the Slightest Sound*
At the Quietest Word*
At the Merest Glance*
At the Clearest Sensation*

White House Protection Force
Off the Leash*
On Your Mark*
In the Weeds*

Firehawks
Pure Heat
Full Blaze
Hot Point*
Flash of Fire*
Wild Fire
SMOKEJUMPERS
Wildfire at Dawn*
Wildfire at Larch Creek*
Wildfire on the Skagit*

Delta Force
Target Engaged*
Heart Strike*
Wild Justice*
Midnight Trust*

Emily Beale Universe Short Story Series
The Night Stalkers
The Night Stalkers Stories
The Night Stalkers CSAR
The Night Stalkers Wedding Stories
The Future Night Stalkers

Delta Force
Th Delta Force Shooters
The Delta Force Warriors

Firehawks
The Firehawks Lookouts
The Firehawks Hotshots
The Firebirds

White House Protection Force
Stories

Future Night Stalkers
Stories (Science Fiction)

The Emily Beale Universe
Reading Order Road Map

any series and any novel may be read stand-alone
(all have a complete heartwarming Happy Ever After)

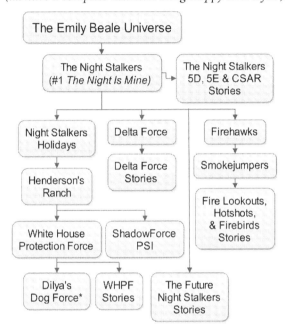

* *Coming soon*
For more information and alternate reading orders, please
visit: www.mlbuchman.com/reading-order

SIGN UP FOR M. L. BUCHMAN'S NEWSLETTER TODAY

and receive:
Release News
Free Short Stories
a Free Book

Get your free book today. Do it now.
free-book.mlbuchman.com

Printed in Great Britain
by Amazon

What God Can Do For You

Michael SB Reid

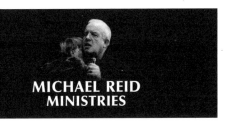

MICHAEL REID
MINISTRIES

Michael Reid Publishing
49 Coxtie Green Road
Brentwood Essex CM14 5PS
England

ISBN 1-871367-32-8

All scripture quotations in italics are taken from the
King James Version of the Bible.

ACKNOWLEDGEMENTS

I would like to thank those who patiently helped me compile this book - Sheila Graziano, Claire Lim, Sarah Reid, Katie Pring, Anthony Graziano and others for their help and input.

DEDICATION

To those dear Christians who have struggled under the weight of conditional salvation, I offer this book, pointing them to the free gift of God in true redemption.

Contents

Bishop Michael Reid

Dear Friend

It has been my joy to preach the Gospel in every continent of the world and to see the wonderful, miracle working power of our Lord and Saviour, Jesus Christ. There is no greater joy than to see people come into life in Christ, to see bodies healed, blind eyes opened, the deaf and dumb hear and speak, cancers wither, cripples run and the rejected brought into the family of God.

Perhaps you are somewhere on the journey to life in Christ - you can identify with the inward struggles and the hurts of life. Maybe you have found what a cruel world it is, how lonely a path which so many walk, how impossible it seems that you could ever get that inward peace and joy that comes from heaven? I want to explain to you just what Redemption means, how wonderful it is that Christ has done it all for us. I want to share with you the depths of grace and the truths of the love of God so that you can share that reality of life and life more abundant.

To my delight and amazement, the publishing of *Faith: It's God Given* and *It's So Easy* has been met with thousands of emails and letters from readers who said the books have changed their lives. This is my greatest reward and has encouraged me to write again.

I very much welcome your thoughts, comments, suggestions and questions. You can contact me with your feedback through the dedicated forum on our website www.michaelreidministries.org/whatgodcandoforyou/, or by letter (see page 98 for my address).

The greatest thrill in life is to know you have made a difference to someone. My deep appreciation to those thousands of readers who have made this dream come true.

Enjoy!

Michael Reid

What God Can Do For You

"O God, here I come."

1

Plucked from the Deep

I t happened one ordinary day in August. I was only six years old; my brother John was thirteen months older. Our family had gone down to the beach to enjoy the sun and the sea near our home in Westgate, Kent. Just before our picnic lunch, the pair of us ran down the slipway from the promenade to play in the sea. It was high tide and the waves were washing up the slipway. My parents were preparing the picnic on the promenade and it seemed such an idyllic day.

At that time I had not learnt to swim but the slipway was very wide and we felt quite safe playing there. John and I began to play under water, holding our breath to see who could stay under the longest. Suddenly, a strong wave washed me away and with my outstretched foot I felt the edge of the slipway. All of a sudden that idyllic day turned into one of panic. The sea was over 12 feet deep. I could not swim and I could not get back to the safety of the slipway. I had my eyes open and saw bubbles of air going up. I knew I was drowning and there was no-one to help. With seeming resignation I remember thinking, as I lost consciousness, "O God, here I come."

It was a busy weekend at the beach and, as it was lunchtime, many of the families were driven to the promenade by the high tides and were busy preparing their meals. Others were sunbathing and enjoying a beautiful day. One woman among the crowd, eating her lunch and looking out to sea, suddenly noticed a little hand break the surface of the water between the waves. She leapt up and dived off the promenade, fully clothed, and swam quickly to where she had seen the hand. She plucked my unconscious body from the sea and brought me back to the slipway. Very quickly a doctor friend who was there helped to revive me. To this day I thank God for that woman who rescued me.

I was not a Christian at the time and had never heard the Gospel but somehow, deep inside, I knew I belonged to God. It was a child-like simple faith, born from a grandmother who had taught John and me to pray when I was four years old. When she came to visit she taught us simple prayers to say every night. Her influence put a seed within my life that would, in years to come, bear fruit. In a very simple way I was plucked from the deep with a heart that was committed to God.

As years have gone by, I realise how Almighty God has everything under His control. A woman, on a promenade on a day out, was observant enough to see a child in distress and acted as a guardian angel. So many times I meet people who recount how God has supernaturally intervened to save them from the most terrifying circumstances, and their realisation that they always belonged to God. It is a revelation to which every true child of God comes. We were *in Him before the foundation of the world.* Everything in our lives proves it. Once we are born again and filled with His Spirit, everything in life begins to make sense and we understand how the hand of God has worked out every detail. The negatives of life become positives when we see His hand protecting us, keeping us and drawing us to Him.

Many times in life we experience ups and downs as circumstances seem to conspire to rob us of what we feel we have. From that moment, when I knew God had plucked me from the deep, I began a quest to find the reality of who God really was and what He was really like. My parents were not churchgoers, far from it. They were totally turned off by church and religion, and only attended for baptisms, marriages and funerals. Yet, somehow inside of me, I knew there was a God who was real.

When I was eight years old, I experienced another life changing event. At two o'clock in the morning, I was awakened by a neighbour. I was surprised to find him in my house. My brother and I did not know what was going on when he told us, "Your mother needs you both to be brave." We did not know what he meant and then he revealed that my father had died of a heart attack just an hour before and my mother was really in shock. Everything became a blur. As a youngster I did not know what to think but I remember the next morning after breakfast, when I was in our garden, I saw a hearse come and take away a coffin with my father inside and the strangest thought occured. Within myself I thought, "If Jesus had been here, my father wouldn't have died. He would have raised him up." Deep inside of me, I had an unexpected faith and a comfort that took away grief and pain. It was not something I could explain to anyone, but it was so real to me.

It is so sad that such child-like faith can be shattered when the wrong influences come to bear in a life. How important it is for youngsters to have the support and love of people who encourage their faith and nurture their simple trust.

Torn from what seemed an idyllic life for a young boy - the sea, the sun, the fun and the freedom of life - I found myself suddenly thrust away far from home in boarding school, in unfamiliar surroundings and a rude awakening of the harshness of life and the loneliness of being snatched from my family. The only comfort I had were the prayers my grandmother had taught me and the God who cared for me, no matter what.

Disillusionment soon struck my soul. The harsh world of self-centredness, competition, envies and jealousies, bigotry and boasting, and the law of the jungle that 'might was right,' began to eat into my consciousness: "How could God allow these things to happen?" I found there was no one with whom to share my inward thoughts and nobody who understood what 'ticked' within. The world had become a place of adversity and rejection. I soon discovered the hypocrisy of the so-called chaplains who had the harsh world of religion but seemed to have no understanding of the needs of a soul. It drove me away from the One who had plucked me from the deep and I found myself denying that He ever existed. How cruel is the world to rob children of their simple faith and trust in such a wonderful God.

A few years after I left school I joined the police. I believed I could make a difference in society and do something to correct the wrongs that were so patently obvious to me. I dedicated myself to really working for what was right. Once again, I found scepticism and corruption was everywhere. People's motives were far removed from what I expected. It was a political minefield and it was not long before I saw the absurdity of our legal system, our prison system and the uselessness of an individual trying to make a difference by putting people behind bars. The frustration of everything got me down. Many a night, when I got home to my Section House in the early hours of the morning, I heard a still small voice saying, "Why don't you pray?" and I would turn over in my bed and go to sleep, angry that such a thought had come to my mind. But grandmother's influence would not die. There was a seed that had been planted inside and it resolutely worked towards fruit.

A moment I shall never forget was when a man filled with the Holy Spirit asked me the most important question of my life, "Do you believe that Jesus died on Calvary's tree and took all your sin into His own body, that He took the power and the punishment of it for you?"

I said, "I've always believed it," but for the first time in my life I knew it inside.

"Do you believe," he asked, "that Jesus Christ was raised from the dead by the glory of God the Father?"

My answer was simple, "I've always believed it," but for the first time in my life I knew it was true inside.

Faith was born in my heart at that moment, so different from the child-like belief and yet so similar. The seed that had fallen into the ground and died, suddenly burst forth into new life. From that moment, it was as though I had never sinned in my life. I did not have a past; I had a future. Everything made sense. This God who had sought me out had finally burst into my soul. I was alive; alive in God and He lived in me. All the scepticism, all the fears and all the rejection vanished in a second and love enveloped my heart and soul. The God of whom my grandmother had spoken became my God, my Lord and my King. Everything in the world was different. Everything I saw and thought was transformed in the moment I confessed the truth of who Jesus is and what He had done for me. I had been born from above by a sovereign work of the living God and would never be the same again. What a God we serve!

My friend, in the following pages, I want to reveal to you that Jesus Christ has done everything necessary to bring life, health, healing and deliverance for every soul. It can be part of your future too if you will just open up your heart and believe that He has done it all for you.

Salvation is the gift of God.

2

What Can *You* Do?

One of the ways in which so many Christians get snared is trying to find a way to produce the reality of life that Christ promised for His Church. So often people read their Bible, looking for the method or the secret to bring about their desires and the Bible becomes a textbook, rather like a Chemistry book. If only they can find the right mix or the right concoction, everything is going to work and the experiment will turn out right. Many struggle from method to method, from fast to fast, from prayer to prayer, from reading plan to reading plan, from retreat to retreat, from church to church, from conference to conference, and yet still come up empty. Rather like the woman with the issue of blood (Mk. 5:25) they have spent all they have on physicians (preachers and pastors) and are no better; in fact, are made worse. If only they could find out what to do, to whom to go, where God was really moving, everything would change. But year after year, their enthusiasm wanes as they find empty answer after empty answer.

The real truth is that they are looking in the wrong place. They are seeking the wrong thing. They are missing the one essential thing. My experience has been that when you tell them so they get angry because their mind-set is: "What can I do? *I've* done this. *I've* done that," and they try to justify all their actions from scriptures (which usually are taken out of context). What they need is someone to cry, "STOP! Jesus Christ is not revealed by what *we* do but by the 'spirit of wisdom and revelation' that *He* gives us."

Let us consider grace, that totally undeserved favour when God *gifts* us life. The Bible says, *"For by grace are ye saved through faith; and that not of yourselves: it is the gift of God"* (Eph. 2:8). The one essential part of this scripture is the realisation that it is not anything that I do but it is *what God does for me.* Jesus died for us while we were enemies, *alienated in our minds by wicked works.* Yet God in His sovereign mercy and love ignores our state and intervenes in our lives as He chooses. The Bible makes it clear that we are born again, *not of the will of the flesh, nor of the will of man* but we are born again of God. It is what *He* does for us. Salvation is of the Lord. The sum total of what we can do is...NOTHING. When you tell a religious man this, he gets angry. When you tell a sinner who has lost all hope and is desperate for help, he lays hold of it with a grateful heart and receives all that God has.

When I was in Kumasi, Ghana, recently, a dear young pastor came to see me. He was desperate to know how he could move into the miraculous. He had seen our crusade and the miracles that accompanied the preaching. He just wanted to get closer to God and to see His miracle power displayed. He introduced the subject by telling me he was on a seven day fast to get closer to God. I laughed and said to him, "Don't eat for a year and you'll be permanently close to Him. My young friend, you don't have to afflict your soul to get close to God. He loves you. He's your loving heavenly Father. He isn't far away. He lives within you. You can't get closer than that. You've just had wrong teaching and bad examples. You can't go deeper than Jesus. You can't get closer than having God within."

It is interesting to note that the great apostle, Paul, had very similar problems with the Galatian church and asked them the question, *"...having begun in the Spirit are ye now made perfect by the flesh?"* It is amazing how many people receive salvation with simplicity as a gift from God - they believe in forgiveness of sins and the gift of the Holy Spirit which God bestows on them freely when they are 'born from above' - and then very quickly they are side-tracked into a salvation 'by works.' They have faith in what they do, rather than in the God who does it all.

Paul asked the question, *"O foolish Galatians, who hath bewitched you?"* The word 'bewitched' is interesting. It means in the Greek, 'to become fascinated by false representation.' When people preach methodology, there is always a fascination in the fact that they can do something to which God has to respond. It is untrue but believed by so many. The Galatian Church was bewitched by the Judaic rituals and started going back into ritualistic legalism to fulfil their legitimacy with God. The truth is: it is Christ's work that legitimises our relationship with God, not some ritual or spiritual exercise that we do. We are cleansed by the blood of Jesus. We are birthed into life by the Spirit of God. Nothing we do will avail, since *all our righteousnesses are as filthy rags* in the sight of God. Why do we go back to try to please God and attempt to ingratiate ourselves with Him? We cannot. Once again I come back to the scripture, *"For by grace are ye saved through faith; and that not of yourselves: it is the gift of God"* (Eph. 2:8).

When I was first converted and baptised in the Spirit, I was so full of joy that it was like walking on air. The Bible became so alive to me. I loved to read it. I just praised God for who He was and what He had done. Some months later, I met a Pentecostal pastor who was shocked to find my freedom in Christ. "Goodness me," he said. "You have to have a disciplined life to be a Christian," and proceeded to explain to me all the rituals I must go through to walk with God. Firstly, a quiet time of at least an hour every morning before I went to work. Secondly, I must read ten chapters of the Bible every day. Thirdly, every night examine my day and confess all my sins to God. Then I had to examine my relationships with people and put them right daily, speak in tongues a minimum of an hour a day, and so on and so forth.

I tried his ritualistic approach to Christianity and soon realised he had brought me under law. I was no longer living under grace. If I failed in any of the tasks he had set me, I felt I was losing my relationship with God. I shook off his whole ritualistic way like a bad dream. I had been bewitched by legalism. I know of pastors in Africa who are told they must fast at least 40 days every year, and some take on a Muslim-type fast for 100 days, not eating during the day, but eating at night. They think it is the way to get power with God. How false it is. My Bible says, the Gospel *is the power of God unto salvation,* not fulfilling certain behavioural requirements imposed under the banner of Christianity.

Two thousand years ago Jesus was born of a virgin. He came to the earth to break the chains that bind people, to set the prisoner free, and to lead him out of the prison house. The Gospel is the good news that Jesus Christ has redeemed us, body, soul and spirit, by what He has done. We were buried with Him in baptism. We rose with Him. We are alive in Him. He lives in us. He is our salvation. He is our holiness. He is our deliverer. He is our Lord and King. He is our healer. He is our sanctification. The truth is that Jesus is everything we need. The Bible says He is the head of all principalities and powers, dominions, kingdoms and spirits. He rules and reigns supreme. What He did 2,000 years ago in His death and resurrection is sufficient for all our needs throughout life: from the day of our new birth until we are caught up to meet Him in the air. He is everything to us. The Bible says, *"He hath made him to be sin for us, who knew no sin; that we might be made the righteousness of God in Him"* (2 Cor. 5:21). Once again, He did it all. What a Saviour! We can rejoice in the simplicity of what He did and He did it without our help.

May you, dear friend, with a joyful heart, proclaim, *"I live; yet not I, but Christ liveth in me: and the life which I now live in the flesh, I live by the faith of the Son of God."* That is the true Christian confession. It is not a boast. It is a declaration of truth.

Who is in control of your ship?

3

Who's your Captain?

Life is like a ship sailing across an ocean. We cannot control the wind or the waves; sometimes they seem on our side, sometimes contrary to us, but we have a direction we are going in. Let me take the example of a great big tanker. It is a mighty big ship and often the waves break right across the bows, and yet the ship ploughs on with dogged determination. The captain on the bridge sets the course and the engine speed and often the ship violates nature's forces to journey in the direction it intends. That is how our lives are. In essence, we set our own course and plough through life's circumstances. The successful people have a will and determination to accomplish what they want. Those who are failures in life tend to get buffeted by the waves of circumstance and allow themselves to be knocked off course and in the end drift with the tide. One of the things to understand about a tanker is that you cannot suddenly make a turn to avoid a collision. The rudder is but a small part of the ship and it takes quite a few miles to change course.

In the Bible, when the writer to the Hebrews speaks about the new life there is in Christ, he said that we need to beware, lest we ignore Jesus who speaks from heaven. We need to become aware of His voice and realise that we cannot plough on in life, setting our own course, because there is literally a new captain on the bridge who has come to set a course for us. It is His will, His way, for His pleasure, and according to His purposes. When new birth happens we lose the right to control the ship and the right to make choices, because one 'greater than us' has come and He determines everything after the purpose of His own will. It is so simple.

In order to live in God's purposes and fulfil His will, we have to come to the place where we stop doing what we want to do and allow God to do what He wants to do through us. So many people try to please God by their actions, to ingratiate themselves with Him. You cannot! The Bible puts it this way, *"And God did rest the seventh day from all his works."* We need to enter into His rest. Entering into the rest of God means that we have ceased from trying to do anything in our own strength or ability. There comes about a dramatic transformation. I am horrified at how many of today's preachers talk about self-acceptance, self-reliance, self-fulfilment, self-love, and just plain selfishness. They do not understand that the life of Christ for a Christian is one of self-denial as a pre-requisite to anything else.

My understanding of Christianity has always been that we are to be 'Christ-like,' having the mind of Christ, having the life of Christ, and having the joy of Christ. Christ confronted sin and the religious man; the confrontation was with truth, the truth of His word. The sinners, who had no hope, heard Him gladly. The religious people, who thought they could do it all themselves, by following their rituals, rose up against Him. When the Gospel is preached in the power of the Spirit, light comes, and the first thing light does is to manifest darkness. No one is going to be happy when darkness is manifest in them; but Christ never manifested darkness without giving the solution as to how to deal with it. Hey! He paid the price for our redemption! There *is* an answer. I would rather have rest and peace in Christ than be lulled into a false sense of security by 'seeker-friendly gobbledy-gook' that puts the ship on the rocks whilst saying that everything is going to be okay.

Wherever I travel in the world I find people hungry for God but totally disillusioned with church. The reason is simple. Many churches no longer preach the gospel of Jesus Christ. They offer life-reformation by following formulas and dogma. Their gospel is a gospel without power but one that demands self-effort. We cannot change ourselves. We cannot live up to Christ's standard. We cannot make ourselves holy. All the strivings of sinners or religious persons will not help them. We need a Saviour who saves us. We do not save ourselves and can do nothing to help ourselves. That is why God so loved the world and sent His Son. The greatest secret to learn is that God knows that if He left anything for us to do, we would mess it up! So, He did not take the chance. He did it all and He left us salvation as a gift. What a wonderful God!

When I was a young man and newly born again I just overflowed with joy. There was nothing that God had not done for me. Why, He became everything to me. He changed my mind, my heart, my soul, my spirit and gave me rest for my soul. It was like walking on air. It was a carefree life because it was His life. I went to stay in a home in the north of England. One of the guests in the house was an ex-missionary from India. She was in her fifties and exuded every attribute of religion that anyone could imagine - she was utterly and inconsolably miserable. I felt so sorry for her when I realised she had spent years on the mission field and ended up in total frustration. I could not help singing and laughing. I was alive.

I shall never forget, after a couple of days, she caught hold of my arm and said to me, "Young man, it's not natural to be happy all the time."

In the world and the spirit of the world we are governed by our circumstances. Our joy and rest and our sadness and turmoil are governed by the circumstances that surround us at any time. However, when we come to Christ, we get a new spirit, a new heart, a new soul, the mind of Christ, and the joy of God. We are like that huge tanker that sails through life; whether the sea is calm or we are in the midst of a storm, we plough through, with the joy of the Lord and the glory of God flooding our souls. Remember when Jesus had sent His disciples to go over to the other side of Galilee? He came walking on the water, in the midst of a *storm*, and was going to pass them by.

Peter called out, *"If it be thou, bid me come unto thee on the water."*

Jesus said, *"Come."*

Peter got out of the boat and walked on the water. Then he began to look at the boisterous waves and his attention was more on the circumstances surrounding him than on the One who had bid him come. As he began to sink he cried out, *"Lord, save me!"* Jesus just reached out His hand and they walked back to the boat together. Another time, Jesus went to sleep in the boat and there was a great storm. The disciples thought they were all going to perish so they woke Him up. Hey! He rebuked their lack of faith! When Jesus is on the bridge of your boat, He is in control. That is why *all things work together for good to them who love God.* We can maintain our joy and rest in the midst of the biggest storm because we have our God on our side; *"greater is he that is in you, than he that is in the world" (1 Jn. 4:4).* We are not governed by circumstances. We are filled with the Spirit of God and can rejoice in all that He is.

Years ago, a friend and I used to compete with each other to race across the Pennines from Liverpool to Ripon over the Walley Skipton Bypass. The roads were narrow, and full of sharp bends. I was a young man and not that wise. Christ had saved me but at the time I did things that were risky. We raced and timed ourselves. One particular time I remember well. My friend, Dave, was driving the car and I was in the passenger seat. We were hurtling around small lanes and there were stone walls on either side of the road. We were practically flying in my maroon Mini with its leopard skin seat covers. Boy! He was going to beat my record!

As we raced around the bends, I suddenly had a feeling of real danger lurking and I said, "Dave, slow down. SLOW DOWN! There's danger ahead!" He ignored my warning. Swinging round the next bend in the middle of the road, we saw a bus parked ahead on our side of the road. We were coming very quickly (70 or 80 miles per hour) and there was no way we were going to stop in time so he pulled out to go around the bus. As he did so, a lorry came from the opposite direction. I knew immediately there was nowhere for us to go. It was either into the back of the bus or the front of the lorry. I cried out, "LORD!" David slammed on the brakes and the car spun round and round, hurtling towards the lorry. I thought it was the end of our lives. Stone walls on either side, a parked bus, a lorry looming towards us, and nowhere to go.

Suddenly, it was as though the car was picked up and placed in a ditch by the side of the road where, for some reason, there was no stone wall. We were facing the wrong way but gently ended up in the ditch as the lorry passed a few feet from us. The lorry driver was furiously trying to stop his lorry and managed to stop some 50 yards up the road. He ran back, shouting, "There ain't room to do that on this road, mate!" We were sitting in the car rejoicing in God who had saved us.

I marvelled that we had landed in a small gap of 16 feet where there was no stone wall on one side. The Mini was sitting in a slight ditch, and resting against the grass bank - there was only just enough room for us to fit. My car did not have a scratch on it when we pushed it out. How did we stop in a matter of yards, with no whiplash or injury, and no damage to the vehicle? How was it that all those years before, God had caused the man who built that stone wall to leave a 16 foot gap for a Mini that was going to come careering towards it with two young men for whose lives God had a purpose? What a God we serve! He protects us. You might say it was our fault for being so stupid. No. We were just young and lacked the experience to understand the consequences of our action, so God protected us. What a Saviour we have!

Whatever the circumstance in your life, dear friend, I want to tell you there is a Saviour who causes all things to work together for your good, according to His purposes. He loves you. He is so, so good.

4

Where's your Problem?

Often when I hold seminars for pastors and church leaders, I ask them if they would like to get all their problems in the palm of their hand and just crush them to get rid of them. They always say, "Yes!" So I tell them to hold their right hand out in front of them and then put it on the top of their heads. Their problems are between their ears!

The Bible says that we are alienated from God in our minds through wicked works (Col. 1:21). Alienation from God is always in the mind. The Bible says that, as a man *"thinketh in his heart, so is he"* (Prov. 23:7). It is what goes on inside our mind that separates us from God. So many people have a false concept of what God is like. They see Him as a judge: austere, punishing and totally unforgiving. If they do something wrong, they feel God is going to bring some great disaster upon them. That concept in the mind alienates us from God. The truth is so different. Let us go to the story of the talents in the Bible.

Do you remember, the man with one talent hid it in the ground in a napkin? He attacked God's character by saying

that he knew his master was an austere man, reaping where
he had not sown, gathering where he had not scattered seed.
What blasphemy! When he came to give an account of his
stewardship, God said to take from him that which he had.
The real problem with the man was his false knowledge.
Think of it this way, life is a gift of God. The whole of
creation is upheld by the word of His power and shows forth
the glory of God. God has always made a way of atonement
so man can come back into relationship with Him. When sin
broke fellowship, man hid himself from God. God never hid
Himself from man. We are created for His pleasure. He
loves us. How could anyone accuse Him of reaping where
He had never sown when He sowed the whole of creation?
He is Almighty God, the Creator.   What an evil concept the
man with one talent had and yet I find so many Christians
have similar false concepts.

Our God is a good God.   Remember, it is the devil who
comes to kill, to steal and to destroy. Jesus has come that we
might have life, and life more abundantly. The Bible says that
Jesus was manifested to *destroy the works of the devil.* He
has come to turn the negatives into positives. He has not
come to condemn the world, but that the world, through
Him, might be saved. His nature is to redeem. How dare
anyone suggest that He is anything other than a loving God.

Legalism and religion are hard task masters and always lead
to condemnation and guilt;   that is why people feel
condemned. Their own hearts condemn them; God does not
(1 Jn. 3:20). So often the religious man makes God in his own
image and then sees God as unforgiving because he feels that
there is no sense of forgiving in himself. The preaching of the
Gospel is the power of God unto salvation. We need to share
the revelation of God as He really is, not as He is portrayed

by religion. He has come to lift us up, not to crush us or punish us. He has come to give us life and life more abundant, not to deny us good things. He has come to lead the prisoner out of the prison house, not to lock us in a cell of legalism and rituals. Liberation is His purpose. Salvation is His name.

Throughout my life I have found two types of ministers: those who seek to restore and lift up, and those who judge and condemn. Really it is the 'seed of the bond' versus 'the seed of the free,' that Paul writes about in Galatians. The seed of the bond are the religious people (the modern day Pharisees and Sadducees) who always look for faults and condemn anyone who does not live by their standards. They have an austere, legalistic system and woe betide you if you do not conform to their rules. That is exactly the problem that Jesus faced when He walked the earth. The Pharisees and Scribes could not allow Him to walk in liberty, and were always looking to catch Him out in word or deed. I know Christian leaders who have that 'gift' and many so-called Christians who have been brought up with the misery of religion.

When I was a young man I was really enjoying a Christian conference I was attending. The weather was beautiful so during a lunch break the young men went out onto the lawns and played football. We had a great game and went back to the afternoon meeting. We were greeted with frosty faces by old 'grouches.' Our crime? We had kicked a football on a Sunday! How dare we desecrate 'The Lord's Day!' I remember some of the young men apologised to these miserable people who could not bear to see a man smile. I did not apologise. I was not going to bow to their religious spirit. I thoroughly enjoyed my game of football and thought how unwelcoming they made the Church of Jesus Christ. For them, it must be a place of no joy, no fun and no laughter - let us just be serious and sad. Little wonder few young people wanted to be part of it.

I guess it was the same in Jesus' day when He healed the man with a withered hand and the poor woman who had been bent over for 18 years on the Sabbath day. His crime? He did it on the wrong day! What hateful religion. What an affront to God. It is not the way He is at all. My vision of God is of a loving, heavenly Father who loves me so much that He has provided everything I need.

When God first saved me He spoke to me and said that if I gave everything, He would provide. It was an unconditional promise from a loving, heavenly Father. For over 40 years He has kept His word and never deprived me of one thing that I needed. When the church started 30 years ago, He spoke to me and said, "You know what you don't want, now build what you do want." I did not want anything that I saw others had built. I wanted a family, a group of people who would love one another, care for one another and live in unity with one another. I also wanted to see the church based, not on the *"enticing words of man's wisdom, but in demonstration of the Spirit and of power"* (1 Cor. 2:4). I wanted the church's faith to stand in the power of God, not the wisdom of man. From the earliest meetings God did such beautiful miracles because wherever the Gospel is preached miracles happen. No miracles, no Jesus! I realised I had to move out of the concepts of religion, and live in the reality of God's life.

Jesus said, *"Search the scriptures; for in them ye think ye have eternal life... and ye will not come to me, that ye might have life"* (Jn. 5:39,40). Life is in the person of Christ not in religious dogma. Christ *in* you is the hope of glory (Col.

1:27). Paul said, *"Nevertheless, I live; yet not I, but Christ liveth in me: and the life which I now live in the flesh I live by the faith of the Son of God"* (Gal. 2:20). It is His life *in* you that is everything. Without Him you can do nothing. You need to abandon your efforts and to rest in the One who did it all.

The Bible says, *"For he hath made him to be sin for us, who knew no sin; that we might be made the righteousness of God in him"* (2 Cor. 5:21). Righteousness is relationship brought about by the shed blood of Jesus Christ when He laid down His life 2,000 years ago while we were enemies of God. It is not what we do. The Bible says, *"But of him are ye in Christ Jesus, who of God is made unto us wisdom, and righteousness, and sanctification, and redemption"* (1 Cor. 1:30). He is our redemption. He is our holiness. He is our life. He is everything to us. He becomes that because of what happened 2,000 years ago. Today He *gifts* us His life when we are born again. He is the author and finisher of our faith. He is the source of all life. He is our Redeemer, our Saviour, our Lord, and our King. There is nothing that He has not done and because of that we can live in the full benefit of everything He has given us. What a Saviour!

All over the world there are people holding 'Deeper Life' conferences. How can you go deeper than Jesus? Either you have *all spiritual blessings*, that Paul writes about in Ephesians, or you do not. There is no greater life than the life of God which we receive when we are born again. The only people that need a second blessing are those who did not get blessed the first time. When He comes, everything changes, and we are brought into relationship with Him. Many pastors all over the world are looking for the latest gimmicks to keep their people and bring new people into their churches. What they really need is a new life that moves in the power of God's Spirit. What people really need to see is the miracle working God. What they do not need are gimmicks that promise people life but in essence only give hyper-emotionalism.

Jesus Christ came to give you a sound mind. He came to bring you rest for your soul. He came to give you the peace of God that passes all understanding. He certainly did not come to make you an emotional freak show, jumping up and down, screaming in tongues, falling over and behaving in an absurd manner. Any normal person would consider that crazy. You need to get back to the simplicity of life in Christ and the glories of our wonderful God. Your Saviour saved you because of what He did, *not* because of what you do.

I am surprised how many pastors quote Old Covenant scriptures and do not understand that there is a New Covenant that Christ sealed with His own precious blood. In this Covenant there is redemption through *His* work, not ours. In the New Covenant He gives us His life within. He puts His Spirit within us. Both Father and Son come to abide in us. We are filled with the life of God. It is all a gift. As the scripture says, *"By grace are ye saved through faith; and that not of yourselves: it is the gift of God. Not of works, lest any man should boast"* (Eph. 2:8,9). Yet I find pastors all around the world putting great burdens upon people; telling them to fast and pray, to plant 'seed faith' gifts in order to get healed, putting upon them great burdens. Jesus said that it is all free. He paid the price so that we do not have to. He did it all. He said it was finished. It is terrible to think that so many pastors do not tell people the truth. Salvation is of God. He is the author. He writes it in the heart and mind. He has purchased us with His own precious blood. What a Saviour!

It is so beautiful to see blind eyes open, cancers wither, cripples get up and walk and to watch the expression of joy on people's faces when they suddenly realise it is a gift! To watch those faces, as the glory of the grace of God meets their need, makes all the trials and difficulties of life worth facing. To see the love of God shed abroad in people's hearts by the Holy Spirit, and to see the transformations that come about when they stop trying to do it themselves, is the most wonderful sight on earth. Salvation is of God.

So often, I see relief come on people's faces when they come out for prayer for healing at our church when I tell them, as I do you, dear friend, "Jesus has done it all. You don't need to do anything. You can't heal yourself. You can't deliver yourself and you certainly can't help yourself. Now, just rest; what God does will get done, and what He doesn't do won't get done."

Did you know Jesus dealt with your past?

5

Who's to Blame?

O ne of the real curses of the modern church has been a proliferation of the blame culture. Christian counsellors have taught people that their past experiences are really to blame for their present problems. So, when a Christian hits real problems in life, the Christian counsellors want to delve into their past and explain that the responsibility for the problems lies in what happened in their past; for example, the way they were treated by people, misunderstandings, family rejection, abuse. They hang their hat on the notion: "It's not really my fault."

A funny thing happened to me when I joined a university course. I was asked to fill in a personal profile, which would enable the lecturers to more fully understand what made me 'tick.' One of the sections was on my relationship with my father.

They asked, "Did I fish with him when I was in my teens?" The answer was, "No."

"Did I play sport with him in my adolescent years?" "No."

"Did I communicate with him and share my problems with

him?" The answer was, "No."

"Did we go to see football matches together?" "No."

The questions went on and there were about 20 altogether, all of which received a "No" reply. Off went my paper, with many others, to the psychologist. When it came to appraising my answers, it was suggested that I had come from a somewhat dysfunctional family background and therefore would be sexually repressed, since I had no relationship with my father. When they asked me about it I pointed out to them that the reason I had no relationship with my father in my teenage years was that he died when I was eight years old so all the questions they asked were irrelevant in my situation. They never bothered to ask if he was alive! So much for that psychological assessment!

People are often trapped into being branded a certain type of person because of isolated information which never reveals the whole picture. Every one of us, looking back at our lives, can think of experiences which were somewhat horrific. We all go through life being battered by circumstances which are not in our control and yet it is our reaction to them which will eventually determine whether they are positive or negative influences.

However, when God meets a man or woman, the first thing that happens in their life is a total transformation - body, soul and spirit - that changes everything. Suddenly they are no longer the person they were born and every past experience loses its power over their future. I tell people who are born again, that from the moment of new birth they do not have a past, they have a future. You cannot change yesterday, but you can live differently from now on.

A fine example of what I am talking about occurred in the

early days of our church. At one meeting, a woman, whom I had never seen before, arrived and sat on the front row. She looked very depressed and smelt like a stale ashtray. She listened to the simple Gospel message that was preached, and responded to the altar call at the end of the service. I found out after the meeting that she had been a 'wino,' who could not start the day without at least half a bottle of wine. She was also a chain smoker (smoking some 60 cigarettes a day). Her home situation was terrible and her children were maladjusted. Drunkenness was her way of coping with life.

Her second marriage was a disaster. She and her husband screamed at each other most of the time and the neighbours got a running commentary of their battles, whether they wanted to hear them or not. That night, God sovereignly met her and totally delivered her from her drink habit, and the very desire to smoke vanished. Inside, her life changed. She went home from the meeting a new woman.

Her husband felt unable to cope with such a drastic transformation and, in a rage, smashed all the china in the house and threw a saucepan of boiling water through the kitchen window. He was out of control. So his dear wife decided that since God had changed her, he could also change her husband! She brought him along to the next meeting and they sat on the front row. He laughed the whole meeting long and ridiculed all the truths of God; yet, he had to admit that his wife was totally changed. He knew something had happened to her but he could not explain it.

The next meeting, she brought her husband again and this time there was a totally different reaction. He cried the whole meeting long and at the end he came forward and asked Jesus to save him. What a transformation! Everything changed in his life. A couple of days later, a neighbour confided to his wife that she was sorry her husband had walked out on her. She could not understand how the neighbour could have got such a strange idea, until the neighbour explained, "I haven't heard him shouting and throwing things, so I thought he'd left." She shared how Jesus had transformed their lives and set them totally free in a very sovereign way. They started a totally new life when they met with Jesus Christ, but the one thing they did not do was delve into their past.

The Bible says we are to forget those things which are behind. We are new creations in Christ. *Old things are passed away...all things become new and all things are of God,* who, in Christ Jesus, has reconciled us to Himself. The new life we receive in Christ is a very immediate life, which depends on Christ coming and living in us so we can say with Paul the apostle, *"I live; yet not I, but Christ liveth in me: and the life which I now live in the flesh I live by the faith of the Son of God"* (Gal. 2:20). Salvation is of God. I tell people, "He doesn't want your stinking life. He wants to give you His life." It is a wonderful life that transforms, cleanses and totally redeems, body, soul and spirit. And it is nothing to do with us. It is what Christ did for us 2,000 years ago, and what He does for us every moment of every day. *By grace are ye saved through faith; and that not of yourselves: it is the gift of God.* What a wonderful gift!

About two months after this woman had come to church and been transformed, she brought her son who was having terrible nightmares and was extremely violent. Truthfully, he had become this way by seeing the violence in his own home and living in an atmosphere of hatred and animosity. Now, everything had changed and he could not cope with the transformation and became more disturbed than ever. I prayed for him and immediately the nightmares stopped. His temper tantrums ceased and he became calm and rational. Jesus Christ is the answer to every need. He meets us in our innermost beings and transforms our lives. There is no one like Him. He is the Saviour of the whole world.

One thing I would like to point out is that 30 years later the family is still going on with Christ and never once did they backslide or have problems with their previous bondages. They found the reality that *"If ye continue in my word, then are ye my disciples indeed; and ye shall know the truth, and the truth shall make you free"* (Jn. 8:31,32). Their lives are a testimony of the wonderful grace of God.

Often, I see people try to deal with alcoholics and chain smokers and people with emotional problems. They try to explain how the problem occurs by investigating their past, thinking that it will help them to cope with their life if they understand how their problems occurred. Christians, on the other hand, do not need to do that at all. Whenever Jesus met people with great needs, He was not interested in their past, only their present and future. He often said to the sick, "Your sins are forgiven you," when they had not asked to be forgiven. He did not enquire into what their sins were, and He did not demand confession. He merely forgave them instantly and healed their bodies.

He is the same today! It does not matter how you got into your problem and it is pretty irrelevant what it is. What you need to know is that there is a Saviour, whose name is Jesus. He became sin, *who knew no sin; that we might be made the righteousness of God in Him.* He dealt with everything and He is a glorious Saviour. It is not what you do but what He has done for you that makes the change. When you believe the good news of the Gospel, you gain the benefits of what He did for you 2,000 years ago. He did it all and you can live in the fullness of it right now. It is the most wonderful truth. He can meet you right where you are. He is the same yesterday, today and forever.

When Buddha doesn't have the answer...

6

Jesus or Buddha?

One of the prevalent practices in evangelical circles is to ask people to come and 'give their lives to the Lord,' to 'lay down their lives,' to 'surrender their lives,' to 'give their hearts to Jesus,' and many other phrases which can only be interpreted as God needing us. People are told that you have natural gifts that God can use and God cannot accomplish His purposes without you. It all seems so right but unfortunately it is all so wrong. The emphasis on what I can do for God is very false, and I want to explain how wrong it is.

Often in a meeting, I will tell people, "God does not want your stinking life. You were born totally perverse and reprobate. The human heart is deceitfully wicked above *all* things. He doesn't want your heart." Then I pause. You can see the shock on people's faces. Only then do I qualify by saying, "He doesn't want your rotten life. He comes to give you *His* life. He wants you to be a partaker of His nature. Christ in you is the hope of glory. It's not what you can do for God. It's what God has done for you!"

Wow! What a relief! The Bible does not teach that I have

to measure up to some standard, achieve some great spiritual height, and become something I was never born to be. Not at all! Scripture records throughout how God digs us out of the miry clay and sets our feet upon a rock. He has come to redeem us, body, soul and spirit. We are born again, not *of the will of the flesh, nor of the will of man, but of God.* Jesus Christ is *the author and finisher of our faith.* He is called the *Alpha and Omega.* Without Him we can do nothing. He is the Saviour and Lord. I just want to thank Him for all He has done.

In my teenage years, I went to a public school where we had chapel every morning. There came a time when I wanted to really meet with God. There was a longing in my heart to find the reality of His life. It was hard to explain to people what it was that worked within me, but somehow I felt that God had to be more real than He was portrayed in the chapels. I tried to reach out to Him. How disillusioned I was, talking to clergy who only had the concept of religion, without the living encounter with Christ. I am sad to say that I got completely turned off from the things of God when I saw the hypocrisy. It just made me angry realising they did not know any better than I.

In my last 40 years as a Christian, I have met so many people who went through the same frustrations I went through as a young lad and came out disillusioned because they felt the impossibility of God reaching them. Often we go through experiences in life which actually bring us to an end of ourselves so that we can respond to a God who does everything for us.

I well remember years ago being asked by a good friend, Alf Schulters, to help at a Christmas house party for overseas students from different universities. My wife and I went to

Capernwray in the Lake District with approximately 80 overseas students from Leeds University. Our first child, Rachel, was six months old at the time. We felt it was a good opportunity to share Christ with people with a variety of religious backgrounds, who would otherwise have been alone at Christmas time. We went on walks during the day and had meetings in the evening, which we encouraged the overseas students to attend. Alf called me his 'sheepdog,' since I managed to persuade most of the overseas students to come. What a diverse group they were. I particularly remember the two students from Outer Mongolia. They had never heard the Gospel and knew nothing of Jesus and His wonderful saving grace. It was beautiful to watch them open up to the gospel of Jesus Christ and respond to Him from a totally atheistic background. What a blessing! Unfortunately, when they got back to Leeds University, the Embassy summoned them and shipped them back to China because they had attended Christian meetings. But I know they came to a living faith in Christ.

There was also a beautiful Buddhist couple who had come to the house party. They were Asians and had a high moral code and considered themselves deeply religious. When the Gospel was preached to them they responded at a very shallow level. One afternoon, on the walk, they asked to speak to me. I shared how Jesus Christ had met me, transformed my life, and set me free. They said that Buddhism had brought them tranquility; they said they had deep peace and contentment. They seemed unreachable.

I turned the conversation to talk about sin and how our best efforts could not meet God's demands and how our desires often drove us no matter how we tried to live. I spoke of the inward heart, our thoughts, our emotions, how anger could rise because of what people did, how tranquility without knowing forgiveness was a false thing. Finally, the young man turned to me and said, "Michael, you're not being fair. Every person has conflict within. You know deep down inside things are wrong but everyone feels that way."

I smiled and said, "That's where Jesus and Buddha part company. Jesus Christ breaks the power of those drives within. He looses the fetters. He brings a deep peace and we become partakers of a divine nature, not ours but His. It's not how we struggle and strive to attain but it's His life coming inside of us and transforming us into what He wants us to be. In Buddhism, meditation cannot bring freedom. Buddha died saying he yet sought the truth. Jesus said that He is the Truth. Christians know Him who is true and are totally set free from the power of sin. We know we are forgiven. We know we are going to heaven and we taste of its powers in this life. Jesus heals the sick and delivers the captive. It's so wonderful to have a God who meets every need. It's not us meeting *our* needs. It's Jesus Christ, our Lord and Saviour being everything we need."

They looked at me and both began to cry. God met them in a beautiful way when they realised that Jesus had taken all their sin, divided it from them, *as far as the east is from the west.* At that moment they started a new life in Christ. What trophies of grace they became.

By the end of that house party, about 60% of the students had found a reality in Christ, just by the simple declarations of the Gospel. The only violent opposition came from two students from Malaysia and a theological lecturer who was legalistic in the extreme. He found the free grace we offered highly offensive. His gospel was one of drudgery and hard work instead of the simplicity of Christ having done it all.

What freedom we have in Christ!

Well do I remember the famous Charles Wesley hymn:

> *O for a trumpet voice,*
> *On all the world to call!*
> *To bid their hearts rejoice*
> *In him who died for all;*
> *For all my Lord was crucified,*
> *For all, for all my Saviour died!*

Oh, to reach the world. When I was first married I worked in Liverpool. I remember how often in the summer I would sit and watch people go by, knowing that for some, life was so empty and meaningless. They scraped out an existence with little purpose and no hope. Time and again, I would meet with those in self-despair who wanted any answer, just something to help them through life. What a tragedy that they had not found the secret of life and life more abundant. It was a joy to see so many met by the sovereign grace and mercy of God. Who but He could reach such empty souls?

> *His name the sinner hears,*
> *And is from sin set free;*
> *'Tis music in his ears,*
> *'Tis life and victory;*
> *New songs do now his lips employ,*
> *And dances his glad heart for joy.*

Christianity is a faith that works in your life. The Bible says that *we are His workmanship, created in Christ Jesus unto good works, which God has before ordained that we should walk in them.* God has worked out a path for your life. He cares so much for you; He has left nothing to chance. You were in Him before the foundation of the world. You can have confidence in His power and love. You never need to strive to appease or please our God. He loves you!

Benson Idahosa was like an Old Testament prophet
with a New Testament faith and understanding

7

Enlarge your Vision

I remember well my first trip to Nigeria to visit the work of the late Archbishop Benson Idahosa at the Church of God Mission in Benin. Archbishop Idahosa was a very good friend of mine, and had told me that if I did not visit Benin with him, he would not visit us in Brentwood anymore! He felt I needed to see what God had done in Nigeria so that my vision would be enlarged.

So many people lack real faith and the ability to see beyond the present. They live with a defeatist attitude and think small. It is so necessary to see success and allow it to inspire you and to take on the challenge. Such was my experience in Nigeria. I saw over 40,000 pastors and elders from over 18 countries around Africa come to join in open air meetings in Benin for one week. I was amazed at the 1,500 people in the choir, the professionalism of the music in the church and the crowds that flocked on the Sunday to hear the word of God. My response to what I saw was to say, "If God can do it here in Africa, surely He can do it in England, or anywhere in the world?"

During his lifetime, Archbishop Benson Idahosa established

over 6,000 churches with 7.5 million members throughout the world. He was used of God to raise 14 people from the dead and had a miraculous ministry which no one could deny. He visited over 149 different nations to preach the Gospel and poured out his life for the ministry. He was one of the most gentle men I have ever known, and yet strong in the power of God's Spirit. I shall never forget seeing him sitting in his office at Benin with over 200 people waiting to see him. He spent time talking to each one, praying with them and often reaching into his pocket to give them money to help them. He had time for the lowliest and cared about each individual. What made him so different from so many modern day evangelists was that he would go amongst the crowd and talk to each one of them. He was accessible, available, and full of love for the individual. For me, he was closer than a brother, and I thank God that He brought Benson into my life.

Let me tell you what happened at one conference I attended in Benin. The 30,000 capacity Faith Miracle Centre was packed; the gangways full. No one else could get into the building that afternoon. Everyone had come to hear the word of God. In the midst of the excitement, there was a disturbance at the back of the hall. Someone was trying to push in but there was no way to get inside the building. The Archbishop noticed the disturbance and stopped the meeting to ask what was going on. The report that came back was that the wife of one of the pastors had brought her four year old son from the hospital. He had died of an asthmatic attack some four hours earlier and she had brought the corpse to ask the Archbishop to pray for him.

There was no way to pass through the crowds so the little boy was passed over the heads of the people up to the platform. The Archbishop took the lifeless corpse into his arms, blew in his face three times and then stood him up on the pulpit. To the amazement and joy of all present, life came back into the little boy and he was totally healed and returned to his joyful mother. Three doctors had been unable to help with his asthma and he had died in the hospital emergency room. Yet three times the Archbishop blew in his face and life returned. I know: I was there, along with some 30 people from my church, when it happened.

Archbishop Benson Idahosa was an unusual man, respected by all, misunderstood by many and feared by the government of Nigeria. I think my good friend, TL Osborn (evangelist and founder of OSFO International), described the Archbishop best when he said, "Truly, he was like an Old Testament prophet with a New Testament faith and understanding." Presidents shook in his presence and when he spoke, he spoke as a man with authority. He had an amazing ability to control large crowds and minister the word of God with such power, demonstrating it with miracles following.

One time we travelled together to a conference in Amsterdam, Holland. Whilst the Archbishop was preaching, a young lady began screaming and fighting and fell to the floor. Local pastors rushed to hold her down and tried to cast demons out.

Suddenly, I heard the Archbishop shout, "LEAVE HER ALONE! Get away from her."

The pastors looked up, shocked. He repeated the instruction. Then he said to the woman on the floor, "Get up and come here."

She came to the front of the crowd and he said, "Get down on the floor and stay there and keep quiet. The scripture says, 'On your belly you shall go all the days of your life.' Now get down and shut up."

The woman obeyed and lay there without a murmur. The Archbishop continued preaching and, once in a while, she would begin to stir and the Archbishop would merely say, "Get where you belong." He preached a tremendous sermon and told everyone in the meeting that his secret was never to give the devil attention otherwise he would give you direction.

When he had finished preaching, he turned round to me and said, "Dr Reid, pass me that jug of water."

He took the jug, walked to where the woman lay, told her to look up, and threw the water in her face, saying, "Go home. You're healed and totally delivered." She got up and left.

She had big sores and blisters all over her body and wore a wig as she had clearly lost all her hair. She was totally out of control in the meeting, and yet, one word from the Archbishop had stilled her. Some three months later, I was taking a meeting near Rotterdam and this same woman turned up to come and talk to me. What a transformation! Truly the Lord had totally healed her. Her skin was like a baby's skin. Her hair was growing naturally, her eyebrows and eyelashes had re-grown, and she had come to a living faith in Jesus Christ. She told me that her previous Pentecostal church had thrown her out because she had gone somewhere else to get healed. How tragic! She was intent on going to Bible College and learning the truths about the things of God. It took a man of apostolic authority to speak the word and throw the water! Such was the Archbishop...but what fruit it bore.

We often travelled together to different nations to minister and it was always a time of joy and encouragement. He was such a man of God. He was so full of fun, joy just flowed out of him and it was so easy to fellowship with him. He had no airs and graces. He was what he was, whether inside the pulpit or out - truly, a man of whom the world was not worthy. Our response to such people determines their benefit to us. To me, he was an inspiration, provoking me to believe God for greater things. However, I found so many other ministers were afraid of him and could not cope with his naturalness and forceful manner. To them, he was a threat and a competition. I was so grateful that he came to our church, at least four or five times a year, since my belief has always been that we should *covet earnestly the best gifts.* It is so important to get the best ministers gifted in the things of God to come and share with the people to plant eternal things in their lives.

Let me challenge you, dear friend, never to be afraid to seek out those who are pillars in the Church of God. Find men who have done at least twice as much as you have, and will challenge you. Never hide in the midst of your peers but find 'fathers in the faith' who have succeeded and proved their ministry. As Paul rightly said, "*…my preaching was not with enticing words of man's wisdom but in demonstration of the Spirit and power.*" Without that demonstration of power, we merely have another philosophy. What separates Christianity from everything else is that we have a Jesus who is alive and does miracles. I often tell people, "No miracles, no Jesus!" Wherever Jesus is, and the Gospel is preached in the power of the Spirit, there will always be miracles. If you go to a church where you do not see miracles regularly, you have not really found a church yet.

'Prophets' or fortune tellers?

8

'Prophets' or Fortune Tellers?

Over the years, some 40 years now, since I became a Christian, I have been amazed at the advent of new errors and then their subsequent demise. Let me explain. One moment a 'new truth' suddenly appears on the horizon and, due to worldwide media attention, Christendom gets hurtled into the latest fad. Christian books, magazines and television programmes become obsessed with the 'new truth' and spread it across the world. The propagators become the people of the moment and race from platform to platform to speak in churches and at conferences. Usually, they talk of a 'new tide' sweeping Christendom, which will be the answer to all the Church's needs. Yet it is not long before people realise it was a mere doctrine of men and the wave turns into a stagnant pool.

I remember well going to the Albert Hall in London, and listening to self-appointed apostles vowing to work together 'for the Kingdom's sake.' It was in the 1970s. Apparently, this was going to be the move to restore the 'Apostolic and

Prophetic Movement.' Great swelling words of commitment, loyalty, and humility came from these so-called 'leaders.' No longer was there going to be competition; they were going to submit to each other. As I listened to what they were saying, I turned and said to my wife, "Give them six months, they'll be at each other's throats like dogs." I was wrong. It took only three months!

In the early '70s, prophets rose up who declared that within three years both the American and Japanese economies would collapse and we would be unable to buy and sell. Christians around the country, deceived by this fearful declaration, drew out their savings and purchased tinned food, chemical toilets, and all manner of survival kits, imagining that they were the smart ones.

I visited a house in Bradford and was amazed when I went into the bathroom to find toilet rolls stacked from floor to ceiling, three deep. I went back into the lounge and asked my host if someone was suffering from a bad stomach. At this point they declared to me all the prophecies about being unable to buy and sell. They had stocked up on tinned food and their loft was creaking under the weight of it. They had taught it in their church and encouraged everyone to go out and purchase dried foods, tinned food and even toothpaste for the coming calamities. They mentioned the names of the prophets who they believed had spoken the truth.

I just asked them one question, "What about what Jesus said? *'Take no thought, saying, What shall we eat? or, What shall we drink? or, Wherewithall shall we be clothed?...for your heavenly Father knoweth that ye have need of all these things'* (Matt. 6:31,32). Surely this teaching contradicts Scripture?"

"No," I was told, "it was a *rhema* word," which I would be foolish to ignore. (They believed a 'rhema' word to be a revelation of God spoken to them directly.)

Needless to say, the calamity never happened and a lot of families had a lot of tinned food to eat.

More recently, a 'prophet' (so-called) prophesied in Ghana that there would be a terrible drought and people would die on the streets. When I arrived for a mission in Ghana, the prophet had already returned to his home in Nigeria. I was confronted with this prophecy by the national television and asked what I thought they should do.

I said, "This man is a liar. I have come to bring you good news, of a good God, who has come to bless this nation, heal the sick, deliver the captive, and lift people up. This is the God I know." I told them there would be no drought and no starvation - and there wasn't.

I could list hundreds of examples of scaremongering and prophecies that people speak out of their own hearts. Often I think they are trying to be fortune tellers rather than prophets of God. They forget that Jesus Christ has come to save us. He has come to give us life, and life more abundant. Jesus said, *"The thief cometh not, but for to steal, and to kill, and to destroy: I am come that they might have life, and that they might have it more abundantly"* (Jn. 10:10). That is the message of the Gospel. It is good news. My God is in control because He is almighty, omnipotent and wonderful. He loves people so much that He sent His Son to die on the cross, to become sin *who knew no sin that we might be made the righteousness of God in Him.* He is a Redeemer and Saviour and has not come to condemn, but to save. What a God we have! How maligned He is by these so-called 'prophets.'

You might ask, "So why do these lies seem to spread so quickly and grip Christendom without real challenge?" The answer lies in Galatians where Paul writes to the church in Galatia and says, *"O foolish Galatians, who hath bewitched you,…having begun in the Spirit, are ye now made perfect in the flesh?"* (Gal. 3:1-3). Once again, it is interesting that the word 'bewitched' actually means 'fascinated by false representation.' People are always fascinated by novel ideas and conspiracy theories. Somehow their minds love to get stimulated by 'divine' revelations that are new, or new methodologies to bring about the purpose of God. It seems the Church no longer cherishes the simple gospel of Jesus Christ, but hungers for some dramatic new experience, some secret hidden key, some deeper revelation, and some method that will reach all needs. And yet, the gospel of redemption is the power of God unto salvation and it is just so simple. Paul wrote to the Corinthian church, warning them not to be deflected from the simplicity that is in Christ.

When I was a young Christian, I found so many people who were looking for 'the Holy Grail;' the secret that would bring the return of the Lord. In the early '60s they looked into past revivals and read books like 'Evan Roberts and the Welsh Revival' and 'War on the Saints,' trying to replicate what other people had done. I remember a dear Scottish Christian man with flaming red hair who read about Rees Howell's experiences and decided that God had told him to become a Nazarene and not to cut his hair.

The dear lad was in his late twenties and grew long hair and a big red beard. He used to walk about Liverpool 8 (a district of Liverpool) and the children in the streets would shout after him, "Hey, Noah, what's happening?" He became a source of ridicule, poor man, because he tried to replicate someone else's experience. Tragically, the sin of emulation (copying what others have done) has become so prevalent in today's church. It does not produce reality. Only the Lord can do that!

I like what John Wesley said, "If it's new, it's probably wrong." The Bible says in Ecclesiastes that there is nothing new under the sun. The Galatian church, spoken of in the Bible, got caught up with legalism, imposing on people methods for maintaining life in the Spirit. Paul made it quite clear that, having begun in the Spirit, we are not made perfect in the flesh. We received the Spirit of God by faith and we need to live a life of *faith*, believing what Christ has done for us. He is our Holiness. He is our Saviour. He is our Redeemer. He is our Healer. He is everything we need. We need to put our faith in Him and not in what we do or how we worship or our religious exercises. *By grace are ye saved, through faith; and that not of yourselves: it is the gift of God.*

So many of the errors propagated today are taken from the Old Testament and used as allegories. Often history in the Old Testament is allegorised and spiritualised to lead the church; but that is false. Although we need to learn from Old Testament accounts, our example is Jesus Christ. The Gospels and Acts of the Apostles are historic books, telling us what happened, revealing what Jesus said and what the early church experienced. The Epistles are the teachings for the early church, and contain corrections for the extremes into which the early church fell. We need to be careful to deal with scripture in the correct way, rightly dividing the word of truth.

Dear friend, let me encourage you to go back to the simplicity of the gospel of Jesus Christ and the truths that are eternal within the word of God. Do not get fascinated by supposedly new revelations which turn out to be misinformation. If it is not in the New Covenant, do not accept it. God's word is a light to your feet and, as Paul wrote to Timothy, *"All scripture is given by inspiration of God, and is profitable for doctrine, for reproof, for correction, for instruction in righteousness: That the man of God may be perfect, throughly furnished unto all good works"* (2 Tim. 3:16,17). Do not get trapped into following formulas sourced in the Old Covenant, because it has passed away. In the New Covenant we have *better* promises and a *better* hope in Jesus Christ. Our Gospel is almighty, powerful, and so wonderful that when people hear it, hope floods their hearts and they find redemption in a Saviour who is so good. Our God is a good God who has come to do you good and bless you and give you life more abundant.

He became totally involved with me!

9

Totally Involved with You

Since we have become an international ministry, we have come into contact with many ministers from all denominations. What shocks me most is how many feel they must stand aloof from their people and clothe themselves with what one would call 'an air of mysticism.' They do not open their homes or their hearts to the common people. Somehow, the teaching of ministry has come down to manifesting gifts of the Spirit, preaching and prophesying, without true compassion and identification with the people.

I remember when I was first confronted with the Gospel by Demos Shakarian (founder of the Full Gospel Businessmen's Fellowship International). He took time with me, even though hundreds of people were in the hall wanting to talk to him; he became totally involved with me. God had spoken to him and told him to "Go get that man. I have a work for him to do." He had the sensitivity of spirit to leave everyone and obey God and devote his time to God's purpose. For the next four days, he had time to help, encourage, and guide me, even though there were some 350 people, who had come to London with him. Demos, and his dear wife, Rose, planted a seed within my heart in those days, that transformed my life and moulded my future. I just thank God that they were so unlike much modern ministry that fails to have time for the individual.

I was at a meeting in Houston, Texas, over 20 years ago, surrounded by some 8,000 people. Coming from England, I was shocked to see how the men on the platform were surrounded by bodyguards. One of the preachers, after he had preached a sermon and made an altar call, to which hundreds responded, just coldly announced, "You're healed. Turn to your neighbour and say 'You're healed.'" He walked off the platform and was ushered out the back.

A dear lady in a wheelchair was at the end of our row and I heard her husband lean over and say to her, "Just say you're healed." She was crying and so was he. I got so angry that the ministers just dumped everyone and left. I could not believe their lack of compassion and care. Afterwards, I went with friends to an Italian restaurant for lunch, but I could not eat. I was just so grieved at the way the poor people had been treated. Jesus Christ had time for the multitudes. He healed every one. He took time from morning to night, praying with them, teaching them, and caring for them. He identified with them because He had compassion on them. My question that lunchtime was, "Where is the compassion of Christ in all of this?" For two days after that meeting I found it impossible to get my mind off the lack of care. I felt those ministers had become professionals and lost sight of the hurting people. That experience changed my life.

"The trouble with you, Michael, is you get too involved with people and their needs. You respond too easily. If you really want people to respect you, you and your wife have got to withdraw from your people and live privately. It's important they don't know how you live. You have your people in and out of your home and you're too familiar with them. To succeed in ministry you have to be separate from your people, otherwise they'll despise you when they realise you're just as human as them;" so a well-known minister once said to me.

I responded, "But I'm a people-person. I can't help feeling their hurts and wanting to spend time with them. They need someone who cares and will sacrifice his time to help them. I am what I am, whether I'm in the pulpit or outside of it. What you see is what you get. Our church has thrived on fellowship, companionship, and the compassion of Christ. We need to bring that back into churches and restore ministers who are true servants, not lording their position over the flock of God."

He replied, "I can tell you; it's totally against the teachings of Bible School. Ministers need to distance themselves from the people. Otherwise, they'll lose their authority."

My reply was, "I totally disagree. If I have to separate myself from the people I love and care for, I'd rather not be a minister. Jesus Christ was always in the midst of the multitude and was always moved with compassion, to heal the sick, deliver the captive, and encourage the downcast. I want to be like Him."

Some 30 years ago, God told me to build a church. His command to me was simple: "You know what you don't want, now build what you do want." I had seen the tyranny of the 'Heavy Shepherding Movement,' and the extremes of the cold Pentecostals and realised that what I wanted most of all was for our church to be a family, a caring people who loved one another. I wanted a people who were available for each other and who laid down their lives for their friends. For many years we had no elders, no deacons, and, incidentally, no problems! It is amazing how quickly a man changes when he is given a title. Position inflates, and it is not long before they forget they are to be the servant of all, and begin to expect everyone to serve them.

During the early days of the church I kept my job so that I was not chargeable to anyone. In fact, when the church moved to a small hall, I paid the rent out of my own pocket. I had to get there early in the evening to sweep the floor and put out the chairs before the congregation arrived. I considered it the right way to lead. As the church grew, miracles happened and people came from far and wide just to receive a miracle. Finally, the church grew too big for me to hold down a job as well and, for the sake of my health, I became the full-time pastor.

Over the years, thousands have come to the church in desperate need of help. Often all they have needed is someone to take the time to listen to them and love them. They do not need cold religious dogma. They do not need formulated solutions to their problems. They do not need self-righteous religious fanatics trying to cast demons out of them. What they need is someone with the love of God shed abroad in their heart by the Holy Ghost. I have found the greatest need in most people's lives is to be 'accepted in the beloved.' They need to find a God who is not angry with them, not condemning them, but has compassion that lifts them up and transforms their lives and circumstances. Above all, they need hope that things will be different and that Jesus Christ will meet every need. They need to hear what He did on Calvary for them; how *He became sin who knew no sin that they might be made the righteousness of God in Him.* They need to know that He is the author of salvation and the finisher of our faith. My God is not demanding that I do something or they do something. He has come with the voice of love, telling the entire world, "It is finished. I did it all for you." He has paid the debt for our sin. He has borne our sicknesses. He has opened the prison house and led the prisoner forth. He has conquered every dominion, principality and power and is both Lord of lords and King of kings. He has come to translate us from the kingdom of darkness into the Kingdom of His dear Son. Our God is a good God and has come to do us good.

One of the secrets I found in Scripture was that Jesus identified with people. He touched the leper. He broke up a funeral by touching the dead body and delivering a son back to a mother. As many as touched Him were healed after they saw how the woman with an issue of blood had pressed through to touch Him. When Jesus asked, "Who touched me?" the disciples exclaimed, "Lord, there's a multitude pressing! How can you say, 'Who touched me?'" Often He ministered to the multitude from morning to night because He was so moved with compassion and care, and said they were like sheep without a shepherd. He washed His disciples' feet. He was full of compassion and care. What a God! What a Saviour! He revealed the heart of the Father, a heart of love and care. The Church of Jesus Christ needs to return to the simplicity of loving people and caring for them as Christ cares for the Church. What we do not need are social workers. We need to hear the word of God, not only in word, but in demonstration of power and the Spirit.

The greatest power on earth is the power of love. Love birthed the whole of creation. The whole world is upheld by the word of His power.　God is love.　God so loved His creation and His people that *He gave His only begotten Son, that whosoever believeth in Him should not perish, but have everlasting life* (Jn. 3:16).　What compassion: to redeem us from sin, from disease and from bondage.　He came to set His people free, because of His great love for us.　The Church must be a living witness to that love and redemption, and then it will see the true manifestation of God's love amongst His people.　That is why we need to be filled with the Holy Spirit, having the power to be witnesses of Him throughout the world.　Our gospel is the power of God unto salvation and the words we preach are not enticing words of man's wisdom but in demonstration of the Spirit and power.　His banner over us is love.　*We love Him, because He first loved us.*　Until we see His great love and compassion for us, we cannot enter into the great commission to reach the lost.

Dear friend, Jesus loves you, and no matter what your needs or circumstances, He has not come to condemn you or blame you.　He loves you.　There is nothing He would not do for you because He has shown it in giving His own Son to die at Calvary for you.　All you have to do is believe what Jesus did for you and put your trust in Him.　It is so simple.　It is the good news God wants you to know.

I know God will bless you.

10

What God Can Do For You

Many, many times when I deal with people, I find
they react against God and against His word.
Their bitterness comes when they find they
cannot get their own way. It is strange how
often people will blame a loving God for their own
determination to violate His will and rush headlong into
disaster after disaster. Often I hear them ask the question,
"Why did God let this happen?" The real question they
should ask is, "Why was I so stupid and disobedient?" God
is *for* us and He is a good God. We need to understand He
is a wonderful, loving God.

We read in Jeremiah 32:33,

*And they have turned unto me the back, and not the
face: though I taught them, rising up early and teaching
them, yet they have not hearkened to receive instruction.*

God's complaint was that those who truly knew Him
turned their back on Him and would not listen to Him and
His instructions. Their whole purpose was to go their own
way. In the Garden of Eden, Eve took of the fruit of the tree
that was forbidden. Sin entered into the world when Adam

also partook of the fruit. The serpent had said it would make them wise and like unto God, knowing good and evil.

The strange thing is that Adam and Eve went and hid themselves in the Garden when they heard the voice of God calling for fellowship. They ran and made aprons of fig leaves. Their problem was that they had disobeyed God by eating of the tree that was forbidden. Their nakedness was not an issue at all, since they had always been that way. The Lord asked them only one question, "Have you eaten of the fruit that I told you not to?" Confronted with truth, Adam again blamed God, "The woman you gave me, she gave me of the fruit." Eve blamed the subtlety of the serpent. Neither took the responsibility that they should have done for their error in rebelling against God's word. It is worth noting that God still sought fellowship with them. They were the ones who hid from God. So it was with the children of Judah in Jeremiah 32; they turned their backs on the true source of help. Yet, what is so wonderful, is God's promise for the New Covenant in verses 39-41,

> And I will give them one heart, and one way, that they may fear me for ever, for the good of them, and of their children after them: And I will make an everlasting covenant with them, that I will not turn away from them, to do them good; but I will put my fear in their hearts, that they shall not depart from me. Yea, I will rejoice over them to do them good, and I will plant them in this land assuredly with my whole heart and with my whole soul.

The Lord never turns His back on His people. In the Old Covenant, He promised an everlasting covenant would be made with them. It is so important to understand the nature of our God. In the Old Covenant He promised in Jeremiah 33:7-9,

And I will cause the captivity of Judah and the captivity of Israel to return, and will build them, as at the first. And I will cleanse them from all their iniquity, whereby they have sinned against me; and I will pardon all their iniquities, whereby they have sinned, and whereby they have transgressed against me. And it shall be to me a name of joy, a praise and an honour before all the nations of the earth, which shall hear all the good that I do unto them: and they shall fear and tremble for all the goodness and for all the prosperity that I procure unto it.

He promises always to do good to His people. His heart is never to destroy but to forgive and redeem His people. In the New Covenant we have better promises and a better hope. We not only have forgiveness of sins, but we have a transformed life when the power of the Holy Spirit comes within, to transform our natures; and we become partakers of the Divine nature. Christ comes to live within us, and the Holy Spirit indwells us in His power. Jesus promised that He and His Father would come and make their abode with us, and this has happened. On the Day of Pentecost, the Holy Spirit was poured on all flesh. He has never left His people. Throughout Church history we find that the Son of God is revealed by the Holy Spirit. Romans 10:6-9 says,

But the righteousness which is of faith speaketh on this wise, Say not in thine heart, Who shall ascend into heaven? (that is, to bring Christ down from above:) Or, Who shall descend into the deep? (that is, to bring up Christ again from the dead.) But what saith it? The word is nigh thee, even in thy mouth, and in thy heart: that is, the word of faith, which we preach; That if thou shalt confess with thy mouth the Lord Jesus, and shalt believe in thine heart that God hath raised him from the dead, thou shalt be saved.

So many churches today have a wrong understanding of what an 'awakening' is. They are seeking to bring God down from above which Paul clearly states is erroneous doctrine. Nor do we have to bring Him up from the depths since He rose on the third day and 40 days later ascended into heaven and now sits at the right hand of the Father. It is a 'done deal.' He lives, and, because He lives, we live. He has paid the price once and for all, for all our sins, and when we put our trust in Him and His atoning work, we find our hearts are sprinkled from an evil conscience. It is over! He has divided our sin from us *as far as the east is from the west* and He declares He will remember it no more. Now, if God won't remember it, we have no right to spend our time in guilt and condemnation.

I make a point of telling people, "You don't have a past, you have a future. You can live different today and the future will be glorious." Remember what it says in Jeremiah, our God has come to do us good. It is so necessary to emphasise that it is not on the basis of what I have done, how religious I am or how holy I am; it is on the basis of what He has done for me. That is why we have called our programme on television, "What God Can Do For You." So many Christians believe they need to give God a helping hand but Jesus said, "It is finished," when He died on Calvary. He did everything necessary to bring us into life and life more abundant. He is our holiness. He is our righteousness. He is our strength. He is our life. He is everything we need, not only in this life but in the one which is to come.

Dear friend, what a God we have! What a Saviour! What a Redeemer! He has given us everything that pertains to life and godliness. He has imparted His life to us and He lives in us. *Christ in you is the hope of glory.* The redemption He brings surpasses everything. He does exceeding abundantly more than we can ask or think, for His great love wherewith He loved us. He has promised He will never fail us, never leave us, never turn His back on us, but will save us to the uttermost. I cannot stress how wonderful salvation is. He is the author and finisher of our faith. He writes it in our hearts and minds and keeps us unto the end. We *are* His treasure. Nothing will change it. Be strong in the Lord and in the power of His might and stand, knowing that not one of His promises to you will fail, but He will bring them all to pass. I know God will bless you.

The most important thing to remember is not what you can do for God, but the revelation of What God Can Do For You!

Michael Reid Ministries

MIRACLES·HEALING·FAITH

MICHAEL REID
—MINISTRIES—

Building on the foundation of our biblically based family ethos, and
our focus on miracles, healing and faith, the church expands under
God-anointed leadership. With the Word of God as our touchstone, we
are a voice to the nations through evangelism, education and excellence

Peniel Church

Founded by Michael and Ruth Reid as a small Bible study group in their front room in 1976, Peniel Church has grown to hundreds of members, with connections worldwide.

Peniel was the place where Jacob met face to face with God. Peniel Church has seen many experience that same face to face meeting.

The Peniel Church congregation is made up of a huge variety of cultures, age groups and nationalities, all united by their belief in Jesus Christ their Saviour. God has intervened in people's lives to bring them together as one huge family with Him as their Father and Bishop Reid as their pastor.

Peniel College of Higher Education

Peniel College is affiliated with Oral Roberts University. Peniel College is in Partnership with the University of Wales, Bangor.

The College's motto is:

Study to shew thyself approved unto God, a workman who needeth not to be ashamed, rightly dividing the word of truth. (2 Tim. 2:15)

This Scripture birthed in Michael Reid's heart the vision for the College. In 1997, Michael Reid was appointed an Associate Regent of Oral Roberts University and in the same year, the College gained a unique affiliation to Oral Roberts University in Tulsa, Oklahoma, USA.

Peniel College of Higher Education is the only campus in the UK authorised by Oral Roberts University and the North Central Accrediting Association, to be able to offer degree courses.

In 2005, Peniel College obtained partnership with the University of Wales, Bangor, enabling students to graduate with UK accredited Bachelors and Masters degrees and PhDs.

The Global Gospel Fellowship

The Global Gospel Fellowship was birthed after Bishop Reid and TL Osborn talked about their own experiences as world travelled preachers. As they fellowshipped together in Puerto Rico they began to discuss the need for an organisation which would encourage fellowship amongst Christian leadership; fellowship that would not only enrich people spiritually but would be a practical help to church leaders across the globe.

The Global Gospel Fellowship was founded in 2000 as an interdenominational forum providing fellowship and teaching for church leaders who believe that the God of miracles still intervenes today. Each year, Michael Reid Ministries hosts the annual GGF conference attended by pastors from across the globe. International speakers including TL Osborn, Bill Wilson, Charles Green, Paul Dhinakaran and Rev V Dilkumar give direction and share at these events.

Peniel TV

"Jesus always took his message to the people and in this modern age, television provides us with a fantastic opportunity to do the same by taking His Word right into people's homes." - Bishop Reid

Peniel's unique TV show "What God Can Do For You" was first aired in 2002. It has gone from strength to strength and is now broadcast into five continents. The shows are packed with miracle testimonies, practical teaching, lively discussion and ministry by the Peniel Choir and are also streamed worldwide on the internet, via the Michael Reid Ministries website.

Peniel Choir

The Peniel Choir started in 1989 with 23 people. Today, it has 100 choristers and musicians, all of whom are committed Church members.

Members range from 18 year old students to grandparents, from housewives to company directors. They are people who want to promote Jesus in song, to support the ministry of Michael Reid and to challenge their hearers with the Gospel message.

The choir ministers weekly at the Sunday 10am service, and travels with Bishop Michael Reid in the UK and abroad. They have recorded a number of albums; see our website for details.

Peniel Academy School

One of Bishop Reid's desires is to ensure that the youth of today become the church of tomorrow. Peniel Academy was started as an offshoot of the church and the aim has always been for the children to become functioning members of God's church globally. The school is open to children of church members and caters for children of varying abilities from nursery to school-leaving age.

Starting in 1982 with a roll of just 17 pupils, the school has now grown to over 150, and its expansion has seen it move to the magnificent 74-acre site at Brizes Park on the outskirts of Brentwood.

The emphasis in the school is on excellence. Behind such a core belief lies total dedication - staff and parents who are astonishingly committed. Their focus is to achieve the best for the children in a holistic way - body, mind and spirit. There is the constant expectation that all children can achieve their full potential in sport, academics and their enjoyment of life.

Most fundamentally, the cornerstone of the school is its Christian belief which delivers a clear moral standard and code of behaviour. Pupils are inspired by staff who are a living testimony to honesty, industry and personal integrity.

Website

The website started as a couple of pages in June 1996. It is has grown to an accumulation of articles, audio sermons, video downloads and much more.

Log on at **www.MichaelReidMinistries.org** for numerous resources:

■ Watch our television programme, What God Can Do For You, online using Windows Media Player
■ Read articles about miracles, healing and faith
■ Podcast downloads of latest sermons to your iPod
■ Search our online catalogue
■ Find out about our next event

The internet has provided another forum to promote the Gospel and spread the good news of Jesus Christ. As visits continue to increase, so do emails of support, questions and prayer requests. Once again, it is a fantastic opportunity to take the Gospel directly into people's homes.

Publishing

The church has always been keen to promote the Gospel through the development of quality Christian material.

Thousands of books, tapes and videos which document evidence of the miracle grace of God, have found their way into places around the globe.

On the following pages you will find some of the products we provide:

Books

It's So Easy!

A truth so powerful, yet so simple that even a child can understand it.

"The most powerful motivational force in the world is the grace of God. Every Christian needs a revelation of God's grace. This book will open your spiritual eyes…read on."

TERRY LAW, World Compassion Ministries

"This story of his conversion and subsequent global miracle ministry is unique."

TL OSBORN, Osborn International

"…A big man with a big personality doing a big work for a big God....This book...will inspire you to reach out to the God who can do much more than you can ask or imagine."

PETER KERRIDGE, Premier Radio, UK

Faith: It's God Given

This book, packed with dynamic illustrations and truths of scripture, is written for those who are sick of the false 'faith' emphasis that condemns and discourages, and will realign your thinking to the true Biblical faith in Christ.

The inspired simplicity of Bishop Reid's message brings a new hope and understanding as he urges his readers to abandon their understanding and accept that GOD ALONE CAN DO IT.

www.MichaelReidMinistries.org

Strategic Level
Spiritual Warfare:
A Modern Mythology?

"Don't touch this, it's dangerous!"

Don't read this book if you are not prepared to examine the Biblical base for your practices.

If you are searching for the whole truth about what Jesus did for you on Calvary and you want to know how to practise true spiritual warfare, then this book is for you!

The concepts and teaching of Strategic Level Spiritual Warfare have drawn people away from the eternal truths of scripture. This book refocuses people's understanding on what the Bible teaches about spiritual warfare, enabling believers to live and walk in Christ's total victory over the devil and all demonic powers, which He won at Calvary.

Michael Reid examines in depth the SLSW movement which bases its teaching on the evaluation of experience and anecdotal evidence.

Order: UK: +44(0)1277 372996 USA: 877-487-4722

DVDs

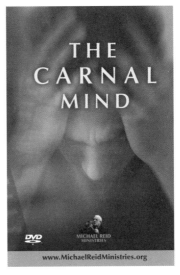

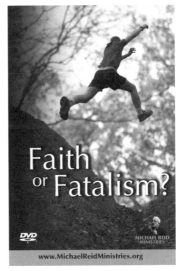

Order: UK: +44(0)1277 372996 USA: 877-487-4722

Audio CDs

The Power of Praise

The Impossible is Possible

The Carnal Mind

Order: UK: +44(0)1277 372996 USA: 877-487-4722

Make a Difference

Michael Reid Ministries is active around the world, providing life-changing spiritual and material help. It is supported entirely by free-will contributions of our friends and partners. For more information about how you can get involved, please visit:

www.michaelreidministries.org/partners/

Invitation

You are warmly invited to attend Church services at
Michael Reid Ministries, in the UK, every Sunday at 10am.

UK: +44 (0) 1277 372996

USA: 877-487-4722

e-mail: info@michaelreidministries.org

UK:

Michael Reid Ministries

49 Coxtie Green Road

Brentwood

Essex CM14 5PS

England

USA:

Michael Reid Ministries

PO BOX 702220

TULSA OKLAHOMA 74170

Dear Friend

I pray that as a result of reading this book, you have realised what Jesus Christ did for YOU.

Please let us know if you were touched by what you read. If you would like someone to pray with you, you can contact us on +44 (0) 1277 372996 or 877-487-4722

Dear Bishop Reid.

Thank you for your clear explanation of the joys of knowing that redemption is what Jesus Christ did for ME and is a free gift.

I wanted to let you know that your book had a real impact on my life.

Special message

_____

_____

_____

_____

Name

For further information please turn over.

If you would like further information from Michael Reid Ministries, please complete your name and address below and send to us at the adddress on the previous page:

Title   _____

Surname   _____

Forename   _____

Address   _____

                         _____

                         _____

                         _____

                         _____

                         _____

Postcode   _____

Daytime phone   _____

Mobile   _____

E-mail address   _____